The blue sedan pulled up and her Mysterious Stranger jumped out. He opened the passenger door with his right hand, a bit awkwardly, but then he bowed with a grace that was as natural as a cat's, and reached in with his left hand to help his passenger. Marissa was not at all surprised to see a blond emerge.

He reached for his wallet as they approached Marissa, but his attention to the girl never wavered. He leaned toward her and chatted, keeping her close with his left arm around her waist.

"A dollar apiece. As usual." Marissa couldn't resist the mild gibe.

He looked at her sharply, just for an instant. The lights from the carousel made his eyes seem to glow neon blue. Then he turned to help the girl up onto the platform, and the moment was gone.

Eyes of a STRANGER

SHARON E. HEISEL

LAUREL-LEAF BOOKS

Published by
Bantam Doubleday Dell Books for Young Readers
a division of
Bantam Doubleday Dell Publishing Group, Inc.
1540 Broadway
New York, New York 10036

Copyright © 1996 by Sharon E. Heisel

Cover illustration by Edwin Herder

The trademark Laurel-Leaf Library® is registered in the U.S. Patent and Trademark Office.
The trademark Dell® is registered in the U.S. Patent and Trademark Office.

ISBN: 0-440-21993-0

RL: 5.5

Reprinted by arrangement with Delacorte Press

Printed in the United States of America

July 1997

OPM   10 9 8 7 6 5 4 3 2

For Carol Ampel,

a dear friend and faithful reader,
who found this book engrossing

Chapter 1

She heard them laughing. She didn't turn around. That was Rule Two. *Never, ever, turn around.* Still she couldn't help hearing them.

Marissa knew from experience that there were two kinds of laughter: Embarrassed and Mean. Embarrassed laughter was nervous-sounding, kind of quick and high-pitched. Or sometimes there was no sound at all. People just looked away.

A voice carried across the parking lot. "Hey, baby, wanna dance?" She didn't turn to look.

"Yeah, we'll do the hippity-hop," another voice rang out, followed by laughter that was definitely Mean.

Marissa knew only one way to deal with mean laughter. She focused her eyes on the ground in front of her and kept walking—very slowly, with small steps. She centered her weight over her right leg, then swung her left leg forward. Brace . . . step . . . swing. She made her way across the mall parking lot, trying to even out the rocking motion of her upper body.

The mall had been crowded when she arrived, and she was forced to park a long way from the entrance. Now she crossed the nearly empty lot in full view of everyone. She passed a pretty blonde who was leaning on a red sports car and gazing into the eyes of a dark-haired young man. They were far too interested in each other to pay any attention to Marissa. That was fine with her. She would have been delighted to be totally invisible.

She clutched a sack from the Clothes Encounter in her left hand. Her right hand found a jacket pocket, and her fingers wrapped around the familiar shape of car keys. A flood of filthy language and more laughter assaulted her. Marissa cringed. New voices returned the abuse and she breathed again. Evidently the creeps around the mall entrance had found new game.

She reached the sanctuary of her battered old Volkswagen Bug. Keys ready, she let her weight rest against the car door as she unlocked it; then she pulled it open and sank down on the seat. She took one deep breath, then used her left hand to boost her leg up and in. She settled back and sighed.

Caressing the cold plastic steering wheel, she muttered, "Thanks for waiting, Prancer."

Hoots and derisive shouts exploded from the cluster of boys at the mall entrance. Marissa chanced a quick look in their direction. One grinned at her and waved an obscene gesture.

She was disgusted with herself. She had broken her own rule and she knew what to expect. Any attention would encourage that kind of bozo and he'd go straight for the sewer every time. She supposed that was where the creeps felt most at home.

Marissa put Rule One into effect. *Keep your head high.* She turned the ignition key and pushed down and back on the gearshift, then backed out. Eyes straight ahead, she pulled onto the coast highway.

Prancer responded to her touch as she shifted smoothly up through the gears. The engine's familiar clatter settled into a purr. She joined the flow of traffic.

Uncle Paul had suggested getting a car with an automatic transmission. He worried about Marissa trying to work the clutch with her weak leg, but he hadn't mentioned it in exactly those words. He had settled for being indirect.

"No need to make it harder," he had said.

"No need to make it too easy," she had countered.

"I'll take some time this spring to fix Prancer up for you, then. I've been meaning to work on the body anyway." Uncle Paul had bought the little car new, more than twenty years ago. During that time, while he was giving most of his attention to his carousel, Prancer had grown as dented and scratched as a cranky old alley cat.

"No thanks. You have enough to do, and I love Prancer just the way he is." Marissa hadn't added that the dents and scratches made her feel as if she and the car belonged together, had not mentioned that when people stared she could imagine they were looking at the car, not at her.

She had let him install a hand-operated clutch last spring

3

for her sixteenth birthday. When the time came for Uncle Paul to hand over the keys, he had had tears in his eyes.

"I wish I could give you everything you wish for, Princess, but old Prancer is the best I can do."

He was the one who had named the car Prancer. It wasn't after Santa's reindeer, as Marissa had thought when she first came to live with him. To Uncle Paul, a prancer was any carousel animal that stood up on its back legs with its front legs pawing at the air. Her Prancer might not be as beautiful as those carousel creatures, but she imagined he was as proud. It was a perfect name for her imperfect friend. It had the right spirit.

It was the first week of November, and remnants of autumn still clothed the hills. Marissa let the bright colors and the fresh scent of pines wash away her last ugly feelings. Steering along the graceful curves, she felt free.

Fifteen miles out on the Sunset Highway, which went from Portland to the Oregon coast, the road crested a hill, revealing a gentle slope down into a broad valley. The valley floor was a patchwork of filbert orchards. Immediately on Marissa's right, a grove of tall Douglas firs sheltered picnic tables beneath overhanging boughs. A lane curved down from the coast highway toward the park.

Uncle Paul had spent a whole summer carving the archway over the lane entrance. On it an ostrich, painted delicate pink, led a parade. In its beak it held a short pole, and from the pole a carved banner streamed back over a whimsical quartet of carousel creatures. The ostrich was fol-

4

lowed by an elegant horse; a bear lumbered behind the horse. At the end of the parade, a merry white cat strutted, its head and tail high. Letters on the banner spelled out SALMON CREEK CAROUSEL.

Uncle Paul earned most of his income carving and restoring carousel animals. The carousel itself barely made enough to cover expenses, but he wouldn't consider closing it or charging more than a dollar for a ride.

"It's too late for me to get rich," he always said with a merry twinkle. Marissa also understood what he didn't say: He wanted everyone to be able to afford the magic of a carousel ride. Besides that, he believed he was already rich, but not necessarily in terms of money.

Marissa flicked on the turn signal and slowed. She always relished the moment when she left the highway and entered the fantasy world of Salmon Creek. The lane dipped and curved in a long half-circle toward the park. She glanced down at the carousel animals waiting in a halo of light. They needed only riders and music to make them come alive. She was home.

Warmth from the glass-fronted woodstove embraced her as she pulled open the shop door. The steady swish of sandpaper over fine-grained basswood reminded Marissa of the rhythm line of a song. A cheerful melody wove around it. Marissa considered it for a moment, then identified the tune. It was a corny old carousel number, "Daddy, You've Been a Mother to Me," Uncle Paul liked to whistle while he worked.

He didn't notice her right away. Marissa paused to admire

5

the quick grace of his movements. Age didn't seem to slow him down a bit.

"I'm back," she said softly.

The *swish-swish* cadence didn't falter, but the whistled tune stilled. Red-orange fire glow reflected off Uncle Paul's glasses as he squinted up at her.

"Glad you're home, Princess. How'd it go?"

The bag from the Clothes Encounter rustled as she reached in. He straightened up slowly, with one hand bracing his lower back, and watched her pull out the dress.

"So-so. This was the best I could do."

Marissa hated dresses. This one was long, but still her leg would show. Shoes were a problem, too. Who ever heard of dancing shoes with a two-inch lift?

It didn't matter anyway. No one would ask her to dance except out of pity. She hated pity more than dresses.

"Nice color," Uncle Paul said. "Your mother used to wear that shade of green."

She remembered. That was what she liked about the dress. It was sea green, like the light coming through a breaking wave. Her mother had looked wonderful in green, especially that shade, which exactly matched her eyes.

Marissa had inherited her mother's eye color and curls, which she had said were the color of a ginger cat. The resemblance stopped there. Her mother had been graceful; she loved to dance. She must have been disappointed when her only child was born deformed.

It was a harsh word, but Marissa believed in facing reality. Sometimes reality was harsh.

Uncle Paul made a sound halfway between a cough and a sigh and turned back to his work. He whistled again, softly this time, and a different tune. Marissa recognized "Nights of Gladness," a song that always seemed to pull the carousel animals forward with its lively tempo. But Uncle Paul's whistle slowed the song until it was more like a melody of longing.

"Nights of Sadness," she whispered too low for him to hear.

She watched him gently sand the horse's outstretched neck, caressing it now and then as if the animal could actually feel his hands. This horse was a stander, with three feet firmly planted on the sawdust-covered floor. When he was restored to perfect condition, the horse would grace the outer circle of the carousel. His fourth leg was raised as if to salute approaching riders.

Marissa stuffed the dress back into the bag. "I guess I'll get busy with dinner. I thought I'd try that recipe for caliente chili."

Uncle Paul looked up from his work and nodded so deeply it was almost a bow. Marissa smiled. Sometimes he reminded her of one of his proud horses.

A bell shrilled.

"I'll take care of it." Marissa glanced out the window toward the carousel and saw two people waiting there. She let the shop door close softly behind her.

Uncle Paul kept Salmon Creek Park open from dawn to dusk, seven days a week. During the heavy tourist season, he hired kids from Franklin Pierce High School to help operate the carousel and the Snack Shack. From October to May, customers rang a bell when they wanted to ride.

Marissa started across the yard. She was tired and her left leg was a dragging anchor. She moved slowly, trying not to look too awkward. The bell sounded again.

Marissa hurried.

Chapter

2

He was tall and dark; she was his opposite, tiny and light blond. Neither of them noticed Marissa. She didn't take it personally. She thought that they wouldn't have noticed King Kong. The young man leaned across the girl, holding her close with his free arm, and pushed the button again. He left his finger on it as he pressed his lips against the girl's. The jarring clang of the bell didn't break his concentration at all. Nor hers.

"May I help you?" Marissa spoke loudly, wanting to interrupt the jangle.

He broke lip contact and smiled in Marissa's direction. "Oh, sorry." His arm held the girl even more tightly. "We weren't sure anyone was here."

Marissa felt a stab of heartache. When she was much younger and played with coloring books, she had always used black for the boy's hair and had colored every boy's eyes blue. She believed in facing reality, but at the same time she didn't see anything wrong with dreams.

9

The young man before her wasn't a boy, but he might have come out of those dreams. She guessed his age at about twenty-three. His hair was raven black. His eyes were a piercing shade that could only be called sapphire.

Piercing or not, Marissa sensed right away that he was one of those who didn't see her. He looked toward her, but not at her.

"It's a dollar a ride," she said brusquely.

The ticket booth was U-shaped and open at the back. A set of keys hung on a nail. One of them unlocked the cash drawer, one unlocked the gate, and the most important key fit a switch that turned on the main power. Uncle Paul had installed the switch for safety, so no one could start the carousel by accident. Marissa picked the key ring from its place on the wall and inserted the red-tagged key in the power panel. The music started.

Then she unlocked the gate. The young man pulled two dollar bills out of his wallet. Up close, she noticed that he was at least six feet tall. His chin was sculpted by a dimple. He dropped the bills in her hand without glancing at her.

The carousel stood under a high roof designed to protect both animals and riders from rain. Skies near the coast range were often gray. When the sun did shine, the roof kept the animals in shadow. In spite of that, the Salmon Creek Carousel was alive with color and light. Each main part of the structure was outlined with round bulbs, and every available flat surface was mirrored. Uncle Paul insisted that the lights be on any time the park was open. As a result, the whole carousel was a beacon of celebration and welcome even on the dullest days.

Lights sparkled, reflected from the glossy animals and brass poles. They repeated from the rounding mirrors that decorated the center column. Each light danced from mirror to mirror, multiplied into a dozen lights, and then a dozen dozen. Each mirror revealed a slightly different view of the couple, like a kaleidoscope image that broke and then reformed, as they moved in a slow circle, inspecting the menagerie.

Marissa had watched thousands of people go through that ritual, walking all around the circle of creatures, choosing just the right mount for a brief journey into fantasy. Sometimes lovers chose the old Philadelphia Toboggan Company sleigh, but mostly it was used by parents with tiny children. Marissa wasn't surprised to see this couple go right past it.

They had a lot to choose from. Standing among the horses were rabbits, pigs, and cats; an ostrich, a giraffe, and a bear. The oddest creature, Marissa's own favorite, was the hippocampus: part horse, part sea horse, part dolphin.

She tried to predict which mount they would choose. The girl looked as if she might be willing to try something adventurous. Marissa was disappointed when she hesitated in front of a horse. It was a prancer with a simple carved saddle—pretty, but not very exciting. Then the girl turned to a proud white cat with its head raised and its tail high in the air. It clutched a silver fish between its teeth. She chose the cat.

He helped her up with his hands around her tiny waist. She

laughed and looked down at him. Their locked gazes held for a moment. He said something to the girl, then wrapped the long leather strap around her.

The safety strap was only necessary for children whose feet didn't reach the stirrups, but Marissa had seen many adults use it. Some thought it was required, and others just felt more secure with it fastened. She had learned to check on the little children and let the adults choose to use the strap or not. He cinched the strap tightly, then swung up onto the horse next to her cat.

Marissa pushed the button that started the carousel. A bell rang and the platform slowly started to turn. The band organ music rose in volume, keeping pace with the animals as they swept around the circle. Slowly at first, then faster, they rose and fell like swells on the ocean. The delicate, tinkling melody of "The Carousel Waltz" wove a garland of magic around the spinning menagerie.

Marissa stepped into the ticket booth, unlocked the cash drawer, and tucked the two dollars inside. The ride was on an automatic timer. It would turn under power for two minutes and forty-five seconds, then coast to a stop in the last fifteen seconds. Very much aware that the counter concealed her lower body, Marissa remained behind it, leaning on her elbows and watching.

She liked to see how people reacted to the music and motion. Some rested a cheek against the pole and stared upward. She was never sure if they were watching the crank mechanism that raised and lowered the animals, or if they were off in some imaginary and faraway place. Some waved an arm in the air and rode their mounts like bucking broncos. Most adults smiled or got dreamy; children, though, could panic at the unfamiliar sights and sounds. She had seen them scream, red-faced, through the entire three-minute ride.

Her theory was that carousels were really for grown-up children. The magic ride brought back the innocence and hopefulness of childhood. A carousel's magic was usually positive. Sometimes, though, especially for the little ones, the magic turned dark. This girl appeared to be lost in white magic.

She reminded Marissa of a Nordic doll. Her blond hair was cut square and short. Her eyes were almost the color of a summer sky. She wrapped her fingers around the pole and raised her face to the small breeze, then closed her eyes blissfully.

Her boyfriend stared at her, his face naked with an almost shocking eagerness. Embarrassed to have seen such a private emotion, Marissa turned away. The carousel coasted to a stop.

She wasn't at all surprised that they didn't say anything to her on their way out. She watched their retreat toward a blue car in the parking lot, their fingers braided and their heads tilted toward each other as if magnetized. She watched him open the passenger door for the girl, leaning forward to kiss her cheek before he closed it. She watched him stride around the back of the car and, finally, she watched the car as it moved up the lane and under the gateway arch to the Sunset Highway. They headed west, toward the ocean.

The girl had been wearing a short dress with a full skirt. She had lovely legs.

Marissa took the bag from the Clothes Encounter into the house. She put the dress on a hanger but left the tags on. It might not be right for her, after all. Maybe she would skip the dance. She was sure she wouldn't be missed.

Chapter

3

He slipped his left hand down along the steering column. His fingers caressed the two custom-installed switches for an instant; then he flicked them both up. *Snap-snap.* It was almost one whispered sound. He relaxed back into his seat. The doors and windows were locked now, and only he could open them.

She hadn't noticed—at least her voice hadn't faltered. Her high-pitched, breathless words blended together until he couldn't make any sense out of them. No matter. He smiled at her and let his eyes go dreamy. They loved that.

She shut up for an electric second, then brushed her fingertips lazily across his knuckles, pausing at the indentation between each finger. Her smile was inviting. He gripped the steering wheel harder.

What was her name again? Something like Sandy, except snooty. Saundra. That was it. Saundra was talking again. They were always talking and they never had anything to say. But

Saundra was suddenly quiet. She looked at him expectantly. She must want some kind of an answer.

He concentrated. She had been saying she should call her mother to explain that they were driving to the coast. She would be home late. Well, she was right about that. She was going to be very late indeed.

A shabby store with three gas pumps appeared ahead on the left. A phone booth stood by itself on the far side of the parking lot. The blue sedan whizzed past without slowing.

Chapter

4

"**Y**ou're right on time, as usual," Cindy said as she pulled open the Volkswagen's door and plopped into the passenger seat. "Why can't you be late like normal people?"

She held a granola bar between her teeth and bent forward to struggle with her left shoelace. The strings dangled dangerously from the right one, too.

Marissa didn't say anything. Cindy always overslept and she always asked the same question. She didn't expect an answer. They had been friends since the third grade, when Marissa, still in shock after her parents' deaths, had moved to Salmon Creek. In the eight years that had passed since then, they had shared a lot of growing pains. Silences were comfortable between them.

Cindy reached over and flicked on Prancer's radio. It hissed. She turned up the volume. It hissed louder. Sometimes it worked but mostly it didn't. She turned it off and they listened to the swish and thump of windshield wipers punctuated by the brittle crackle of Cindy's granola-bar wrapper.

Marissa was about to mention the couple on the carousel;

something about them had stuck in her mind. But the right words stayed just out of her reach, so she switched to another subject.

"I got a dress for the dance. It's green, and it has a long skirt."

"Long enough?" Cindy didn't pull her punches. She talked about everything with a matter-of-fact cheerfulness that Marissa treasured. Whatever the opposite of mean-spirited was, that was Cindy.

"Almost long enough, on me. I'm so short just about anything is long."

"You'd be taller if you stood up straight," Cindy said automatically.

Marissa smiled. She had expected that remark. "I might return the dress. I might not go to the dance."

"I think you should go. I think you should buy a short and sexy dress and just go. If they don't like it, just let them suffer."

"What are you going to wear?" Marissa asked.

"A tent, probably. Mom's going to make a lace tent." Her voice took on an exaggeratedly bright note. "She always says I'm beautiful. More to love and all that. She's making this dress with what she calls an A-line, but to me that's just another word for tent. At least I convinced her to leave off the ruffles."

Cindy was silent for a beat, then added, "If you don't go, I guess I won't either. I don't want to sit in the corner alone. I sort of counted on us being gimps together."

Marissa glanced at her friend. "You're not a gimp. You just don't give yourself a chance."

"Neither do you," Cindy said.

They listened to the windshield wipers for the last block before they got to Franklin Pierce High School. The school stood by itself on the top of a hill. Across the big parking lot was the physical education complex. The people of Tucker treasured a long history of excellence in sports, and that was reflected by the amount of money they spent. The sports complex included an Olympic-size pool, tennis courts, track, football field, and the huge gym, where the dance would be held after Friday night's football game. It looked like the Tucker Tornadoes had a good chance to win another state championship.

Pierce High still kept the feeling of a country school, in spite of now being on the edge of the Portland suburbs. Many of the students had known each other since first grade. Marissa had felt left out at first, but the years had helped people accept her. Those who didn't accept her at least ignored her. But with the area growing, and new families moving in from the crowded city, it was the newcomers who weren't always so kind.

Marissa pulled around to the back of the school, away from the bustle in the main lot. They would have to walk a ways, but it wouldn't be crowded. They agreed it was easier to fight the rain than a rowdy bunch of kids.

"That'll be Rule Three," Cindy said. *"If you can't outrun 'em, outsmart 'em."*

Marissa stopped the engine. The emergency brake made a grating sound as she pulled it up.

She hadn't used the handicapped spot. She refused even to

consider that. She wasn't handicapped anyway. The politically correct word was "challenged." She looked down at her left leg and challenged it to help her get out of the car. It cooperated with a clumsy, but effective, effort.

A few students were hunching over their books and racing for shelter. They didn't pay any attention to Marissa or Cindy.

"Have you ever noticed that some people don't seem to see you?" Marissa couldn't shake the feeling that she had been invisible to the couple on the carousel. "It's as if you don't exist."

"Absolutely," Cindy said. "You'd think fat people would be *more* visible, but half the time I might just as well be transparent." She twisted her lips into a parody of a smile. "The other half of the time, I wish I really were transparent. There are advantages to being invisible."

Marissa looked into her friend's humor-filled eyes. "I'm glad you're not invisible, Cindy."

The school day passed quickly. Marissa usually spent the last period in the pool, swimming laps. Ms. Martinez, the P.E. teacher, had convinced her that it would help to build muscle strength. Probably it did, but that wasn't why Marissa enjoyed swimming. She had soon discovered the miracle of flippers. With every kick, they gave her a burst of power that she never felt anywhere else. She moved in the water with a grace she could never manage on land, not even behind the wheel of Prancer. She was self-propelled, and she loved it.

The only part she hated was wearing a swimsuit in front of

the others, but at least the others were all girls. She had tried to convince Cindy to join her.

"Not a chance," Cindy said. "No one but my mother and my doctor will ever see these thighs."

She had laughed, but Marissa hadn't.

Marissa peered toward the clock through her goggles. It was time to shower and dress. She braced her back against the side of the pool and hoisted herself up with her arms. Sitting on the edge, she reached for the diving platform to pull herself upright. A hand appeared before her. It bore a gold ring set with a large opal.

"Want a lift?"

Marissa pushed her goggles up. Gloria Josephson stood beside her with her hand outstretched.

"Thanks."

Gloria braced against Marissa's weight and helped her to her feet.

"That's a pretty ring," Marissa said. "Is it new?"

Gloria raised it into the light. Fire flashed from within the gem, and Gloria's eyes reflected the flash. "Actually, it's very old. It was my grandmother's when she was a girl. She gave it to me on my birthday last month. This is the first time I've worn it at school, though. I'm afraid something will happen to it."

Marissa felt a twinge of envy, not for the ring but for Gloria's big, loving family. She wondered if Gloria realized how lucky she was to know her grandmother, but she could never say anything like that. Gloria might think she was asking for pity.

21

"It's beautiful," she said.

Her right thumb automatically moved to her own ring finger and rotated the single diamond in its plain setting. It was her mother's ring and was a constant reminder of her mother's love. She thought the ring protected her, somehow, although she wasn't quite certain how or from what. No matter. Touching it was a habit that brought her comfort.

"Are you coming to the dance after the game?"

"I got a dress yesterday, but I'm not certain I'll go. I'm still thinking about it."

"I hope you do. We're bound to win the game and everyone will be celebrating. The Student Council is really pushing school spirit, and my dad is offering free pizza to the class with the best attendance at the dance."

Marissa smiled. She had often thought that Gloria would be popular even if she hadn't been so pretty and friendly. What teenage boy could resist a girl whose dad owned a pizza parlor?

She listened to Gloria talk about dance plans while she sat on the diving platform to slip on a pair of old sneakers. The left one had a built-up sole that made her legs the same length. Without it she walked like someone wearing only one high-heeled shoe. They headed for the locker room, and Gloria held the heavy door open with such casual grace that Marissa hardly noticed.

The locker room always reminded Marissa of the sea lion caves on the Oregon coast, where the animals crowded together on narrow rock ledges, competing for space, splashing in the shallow waves, and raising their voices above the crashing surf. Both were scenes of total chaos.

She escaped into the shower. Five minutes later she came out, drying her hair with quick strokes of a thin gym towel. Something was wrong. The room was silent.

The other girls clustered in a tight knot around a girl Marissa hardly knew. She was a Pierce High newcomer. Marissa did a mental search and came up with a name: Ramona. She hung back and listened, the towel still in her hand.

"They don't know what happened to her. She hasn't been home all night, and they don't think she could possibly have run away because her dad bought her a new car for her birthday, and they found it in the mall parking lot. They think she was kidnapped or something."

Ramona's voice rose in pitch as she spoke; her words spilled out faster and faster until the word "kidnapped" shrilled like a siren. The other girls drew back a little, as if the raw emotion pouring out of Ramona were a physical force. It felt to Marissa as if the air were actually vibrating with all the anxiety. Gloria supported Ramona with an arm around her shoulders and helped her out of the room.

"Who was she talking about?" asked Marissa.

A girl from Marissa's homeroom answered. "Her cousin. She goes to Hoover High. She didn't come home last night."

"Maybe she had a hot date," another girl commented.

Marissa recognized the laughter that followed. It was Embarrassed.

Chapter 5

He pulled into the employee parking lot at Portland Metropolitan University and was glad to see that his usual parking space was empty. It was important for such little things to go smoothly. One break in the routine and other things begin to falter, too. It could spoil a whole day, or a whole night.

Finding his space empty at this time of day was an especially good omen. His shift didn't start until eleven o'clock. He smiled to himself at the private joke. Yes indeed. He worked the graveyard shift.

They actually paid him extra for working from eleven to seven-thirty. The rest of the custodial crew demanded the extra money because they hated working when most people were asleep. But he found peace in darkness. And of course, sunrise was thrilling. Sometimes sunrise was more than thrilling. Sometimes sunrise was rapturous.

It seemed as if an unseen force must be directing his life. He sensed it at work when the little things went his way, like having his parking space available whenever he needed it. He locked the car door and got his tackle box out of the trunk, then sauntered toward the science building.

He had to stop at the department office to check his work schedule. A glance through the open door made him wince inwardly. Joan Parker sat at her desk, facing the hallway. She looked up from her computer keyboard and waved a greeting.

He waved back with his free hand and went into the office. The tackle box felt heavier under her penetrating gaze. Nothing escaped Nosy Parker. She would love to see inside his little treasure chest. Yes indeed. And he would love a chance to show her.

Fighting an impulse to do just that, he gripped the handle tighter and picked up the clipboard that held custodians' work assignments. Good, the animal room needed cleaning. He had a little plan to make that job more interesting. He turned his attention back to Joan, who hadn't stopped talking.

She nattered on about her son, a loser named Steve. Little Stevie was in trouble again, something about fighting with his girlfriend, failing classes, thinking about joining the navy.

He put down the clipboard and tried to concentrate on what she was saying. Evidently his effort showed. She thought he really cared. She talked faster and batted her mascara-thick eyelashes. He watched her closely, quietly. Joan revved up her chatter, then finally got to the point. Would he help, the way he had helped last spring when Steve had had that little brush with the police?

He shrugged. Why not? It was pitiful, the way she nearly melted with gratitude. Her long red nails danced before his vision as he watched her write Steve's new phone number on a Biology Department memo pad. She patted her hair and wiggled in her chair a little when he tucked the paper in his pocket.

He ducked his head slightly. She responded the way he knew she would, with another hair pat and wiggle. He escaped into the dim hallway with her voice following, telling him not to be a stranger, now.

No, he wouldn't be a stranger. He touched his shirt pocket and heard the paper crinkle faintly. Maybe this was something he could use. Maybe, like the parking place and a thousand other examples of his special status, it was a sign.

He wasn't surprised to find the elevator empty. By late afternoon, most of the students and professors had gone home. He expected to have the basement to himself, too.

The elevator rumbled as it descended. He stepped out into a cool concrete hallway that smelled faintly of urine. Rustling sounds came from the direction of the animal room. He stopped at the maintenance cubicle and unlocked a metal cabinet that contained chemicals. He put his tackle box on a shelf and listened for footsteps or breathing, then looked over his shoulder. He knew he must be alone, but still he sometimes felt someone standing behind him, watching.

He snapped the lid open. Light reflected off shiny car keys and a plastic ornament that spelled "Saundra." It had been very smart to keep that. Yes indeed. That was going to be handy. His hands shook as he slipped the paper with Steve's phone number into the box and closed the lid. He slid the box to the rear of the shelf and locked the cabinet, giving the padlock a hard, testing tug.

Each new breath came slightly deeper and quicker than the one before. He hurried to the animal room.

The Psychology Department had finished a series of learning experiments using rats. There was no further use for the animals, so they would be "sacrificed." He liked the ring of the scientist's word. Compared to "kill," "sacrifice" sounded almost admirable.

Usually they used chloroform, but he had a preferred method. People rarely came to the animal room, especially at this time of day. His shift wasn't supposed to start for another six hours. He was sure he wouldn't be disturbed.

He hummed to himself as he carried an empty aquarium into the mop room, then used a hose to fill it with water. Overflow splashed to the floor and ran out through a drain. He slid a heavy piece of clear acrylic into place as a lid.

He was panting by the time he returned with a wire cage squirming with rats. The cage rattled, partly from the animals' movements, and partly from the violent shaking of his hands. Still, he managed to dump the rats into the aquarium, slide the cover back into place, and weigh it down with an empty mop bucket.

Continuing to hum, he pulled up a stool and watched. The animals struggled in the water, clawing at each other and pushing toward the surface, only to find a transparent barrier between them and life-giving air. While he watched, he thought about Nosy Parker and how coy she was with him, even though she was old enough to be his mother. He imagined Nosy Parker in there instead of the rats.

Better yet, he thought, *with* the rats.

By the time the animals stopped twitching, his breathing had slowed and his trembling had quieted. He was still humming.

Chapter 6

"Anything interesting happen at school today?" Uncle Paul regarded Marissa across the kitchen table. He tilted his chair back, balancing his weight over its back legs like one of the boys in Marissa's English class.

"No, nothing at all." It was a game they played often. Now it was his turn to make a move.

"Nothing about the history of the universe or maybe the final number in pi?"

"Nothing of interest . . . except maybe the habits of South American centipedes."

"How about the habits of the dread *Teen-ageus americanus?*"

"Nothing. Nothing at all."

"Nothing about going to a victory dance Friday night after the colossal clash of the Tucker Tornadoes and the Kellingham Kumquats?"

"It's the Kellingham Knights, Uncle Paul. Gloria's dad is

giving free pizza to the class with the highest attendance. It's to build school spirit."

"Will you dance the hokeypokey and the jitterbug? I might want to come."

"I don't know what *they'll* dance." Marissa emphasized the pronoun. "I'm supposed to bring chocolate gingersnaps; Cindy is going to bring punch."

She started to collect the dishes, keeping her hands busy and her eyes diverted from his.

"You have enough spirit to supply the whole school," he said. "Don't you worry about anything. You're doing just fine."

"Thanks," she whispered. Then, because she knew he worried about it, "You're doing fine, too."

He sighed. "I'm not much of a parent to you, Princess. I do what I can and I know it isn't always right or always enough. I hope you'll keep on being patient with an old man who doesn't know apples from road apples about raising a teenage girl."

"It's the first time for both of us," she said.

When her parents died, Marissa thought she would be put in a foster home and that social workers would try to find adoptive parents for her. Even at eight, she knew her chances of being adopted were slim. She was, after all, a child with "special needs." She wasn't so seriously crippled that she would ever need a wheelchair, but there would be extra medical expenses and her custom-built shoes cost a young fortune.

In addition to the loss of her parents, she lost any sense of home or of simply belonging. Then Uncle Paul showed up.

He wasn't exactly her uncle. He was her great-uncle, her grandfather's brother. He had been a bachelor all his life, living alone with his carousel. When he heard that Marissa had no one, he came for her.

"We're in this together," he told her. "I won't be much of a father and less of a mother, but we have each other and I guess we'll make do."

They had, too. At least they had done their best. Things fell apart for Marissa when she had to change schools. The kids in her old school had known her since the first day of kindergarten and they accepted her. Some of the kids at her new school teased her without mercy. Overwhelmed by the teasing and the adjustment to a new life with Uncle Paul, and missing her parents with a tearing ache that sometimes threatened to rip her apart, Marissa gave up for a while and withdrew into silence.

Three things restored her will to keep fighting: Cindy's friendship, Uncle Paul, and the fantasy world of the carousel. She put her arm around Uncle Paul's shoulder, feeling thankful for his warmth.

"You're doing just fine," she repeated.

"Feast your eyes on page one." Cindy got into the car and handed Marissa a copy of *The Argus*, Pierce High's school paper. "They printed my whole article on dances and etiquette in the new century. Maybe this will turn out to be a civilized affair after all." Her eyes sparkled.

Marissa let the engine idle while she scanned the article. Cindy had written that courtesy on the football field was called sportsmanship, but the same idea at a party or a dance was called etiquette. Both boiled down to acting with respect for oneself and others.

"It's a good article, Cindy. I especially like the idea of respecting yourself. It's Rule One, isn't it? Keep your head high."

"Does that mean we're going to the dance?"

Marissa eased Prancer into first gear. "Do you honestly think we should?"

"Absolutely."

Marissa sighed. "I guess it won't hurt. No one will pay any attention to us anyway."

"I'll tell Mom to finish the tent," Cindy said, grinning.

The gym had been transformed. The decorating committee had formed golden tepees with dried cornstalks and had arranged orange pumpkins among heaps of pale straw on the floor. The basketball hoops were festooned with gold, rust, and yellow crepe paper. Someone from the theater department had put orange and gold filters on the lights.

"They make my dress look sick," Marissa commented.

Her dress followed the shape of her slender body as if it had been designed for her. It was long, but she would have preferred it even longer. It revealed some of her withered calf muscle, but it wouldn't show more unless she twirled. She thought there was zero probability that she would be twirling.

"The light is wrong for the dress, but it really brings out the highlights in your hair," Cindy said. "Stand up straight and you'll be gorgeous."

Marissa sighed and straightened her shoulders. She studied her friend. Cindy's hair had the soft glow of antique gold, and the filtered light enhanced her raisin-colored dress. Her mother had draped the bodice in loose folds and gathered the material just below the waist. The skirt was slightly flared and swayed gracefully as Cindy walked.

"Your dress is beautiful," Marissa said. "It is definitely not a tent."

"I guess it's not too bad," Cindy admitted. "Mom has a gift for this stuff."

They stopped at the table where Gloria and the rest of the refreshment committee were busy arranging drinks and snacks. Gloria wore pale blue. Her hair was pulled back and fastened with a sea-green ribbon that fell down to the middle of her back. The ribbon danced when she moved her head.

Gloria saw them coming and smiled. "That's a pretty dress, Cindy."

"Thanks." Cindy looked pleased as she handed over her bag of punch ingredients. Marissa held out a platter heaped with chocolate gingersnaps.

Gloria took the platter and said, "Marissa, I hear you brought some old horror movies for the arts class on Halloween. Do you think I could borrow one? We're supposed to do a movie report in English next week. Mrs. Simon wants us to watch a film made before 1945."

"Sure," Marissa said. "I have the silent version of *Nosferatu,* the best-ever Dracula movie. I'll bring it to school on Monday."

Gloria was looking at her so closely that Marissa wondered for a second if her face was dirty. She must have looked puzzled because Gloria blinked and said, "I'm sorry. I was just thinking . . . Here, try this." She pulled the ribbon from her hair and held it out. "It would be gorgeous with your eyes and hair."

The ribbon was the same shade as Marissa's dress. Gloria came around the table and wrapped the thin ribbon through Marissa's curls, then tied a delicate bow over her left ear.

"It's gorgeous," Cindy said. "Just look." She pulled a tiny mirror out of her purse and held it up.

Between Cindy's approving expression and what she saw in the mirror, Marissa had to agree. "Thank you," she said, almost whispering. She was glad she had decided to come.

Someone asked Gloria a question, and she waggled her fingers in a little salute before she turned away.

Cindy grinned at Marissa. "Attitude is everything," she said, and led the way to the edge of the dance floor with her shoulders back and her head high.

They surveyed the room. There were two choices. They could walk directly across the mostly empty space where just a few couples were dancing, or they could go around the edge of the gym floor, past other early arrivals who had taken the closest chairs.

The dance floor was out. They started around the edge.

Their goal, half a dozen empty chairs, was just ahead. They would have to pass a group of six freshmen boys who stood uncertainly in a row. Four of them had their hands buried deep in their pockets. The two on each end stood with their legs planted wide and their arms folded across their chests. Marissa wondered whether they were trying to look belligerent or to protect themselves. She decided they were probably trying to do both.

The boys formed a brief huddle. Their leader, a greasy-haired brute who wore tinted glasses even indoors and after dark, stared toward the refreshment table and shrilled a jarring whistle. Gloria looked up, startled. He held up both hands with his fingers extended, then folded in one thumb. He whistled again and the other boys laughed loudly.

"Nine, baby!" he shouted to be heard above the music. Gloria turned away, ignoring them all.

"Oh brother," Cindy muttered. "The Rating Game. I hate this!" She stopped abruptly.

Marissa bumped into her and wobbled, trying to maintain her balance. She leaned toward Cindy and whispered, "All three rules apply. Head high, never turn around, and if you can't outrun them—"

"It sure won't be hard to outsmart them," Cindy finished for her, and giggled. They kept walking.

No one appeared to notice them. Marissa thought, with gratitude, that this was one of those times when they were invisible.

Then one of the boys whistled such a sudden screech that she broke Rule Two and looked toward him. He caught her eye and grinned. Then he held up the thumb and index finger of his right hand, forming them into a circle.

"Zero," he mouthed without making a sound.

Marissa, mortified, saw that he was looking not at her but

at Cindy. She grabbed Cindy's arm and tried to hurry her along, hoping she hadn't seen. The glimmer of moisture in Cindy's eyes betrayed her.

The dance didn't get any better. The music was fine. The refreshments were passable. Marissa had two cookies and some punch. Cindy refused to eat anything and barely talked. Lots of other people danced, but of course they did not.

The gang of boys moved on to other kinds of fun, and none of them danced either. They disappeared into the bathrooms pretty often. Marissa whispered to Cindy that they were probably going in there for a brain transplant. That was as close as Cindy came to smiling.

The girls left early. On the way out, they almost bumped into Ramona.

"Have you heard anything?" Marissa asked.

Ramona shook her head slowly, as if even that little bit of effort drained her. She looked even more upset than she had on the first day after her cousin vanished. "No. No, we haven't. The only thing we know is Saundra talked about having some new boyfriend, but my aunt and uncle never met him."

On the way home, Marissa stopped at a little grocery store near the edge of town. "I need milk for breakfast," she said. "Do you want anything?"

"Absolutely," Cindy answered. "I need a candy-bar fix."

They stood in line behind two women and a man, each carrying either milk or bread. "Look at this." Marissa pointed to the newspaper rack.

36

The headline read: GIRL MISSING: ABDUCTED FROM MALL? Beneath the headline was a fuzzy photograph of a pretty blond girl in a cheerleader's outfit. She was holding both arms up in a V and grinning back over her shoulder toward the camera.

"I'd rather be invisible," Cindy said.

Chapter

7

The phone was picked up on the third ring. Steve sounded sleepy. Good. Sleepy people were vulnerable.

He identified himself and apologized for calling so early in the morning, explaining that he was just getting off work. Could he come by for coffee? Steve sounded confused, then surprised, but he was friendly enough. After all, little Stevie owed him.

He carried the tackle box out to his car and put it in the trunk. Then he drove to Steve's house.

The kid was a mess. His hair stuck up in clumps, and his bare feet didn't look at all clean. His apartment stank of sour laundry and moldy food. He offered cups of bitter coffee. They sat in the cluttered living room.

It was absurdly easy to convince Steve that he had come to offer help. He talked about how worried Steve's mother was, how she only wanted the best for him. He owed his mother more respect. After all, she had made sacrifices for him.

He should definitely stay in school and try a little harder to get decent grades. Maybe he should get a new girlfriend, show that he was serious about his future. Why didn't he call that pretty blond girl, the one he had been seeing last spring?

He could see that Steve was grateful for the advice. Kids sometimes needed a little boost to keep them on the right track. Not that he was that much older than Steve, but he was certainly a whole lot more experienced. Yes indeed, a whole lot more.

The mess in the little house almost gagged him. He left as soon as he could. Fresh morning air was as welcome as a cleansing shower, and he hummed to himself as he backed out of Steve's driveway.

Getting into Steve's trunk had been child's play. It had one of those pop-up levers next to the driver's seat, and Steve was not the type to lock his car when it was in his own driveway. It took only a few seconds to open the trunk, slide the bolt cutters behind the spare tire, and tuck the vials and keychain into the tire itself.

The hardest thing was parting with his trophies, but he was sure he could get more. In fact, it was time to begin the next Hunt.

Steve sprawled on the couch and watched the door close. He hated that his mother had sent Nick to straighten him out. She was always telling him he ought to be more like "that nice boy who works at the university." Steve wasn't at all sure that Nick was nice. He thought Nick was putting on some kind of an act, pretending to be mysterious and superior in a way that mothers lapped up and purred over. Still, Steve had to admit that Nick had been a real help in that trouble last spring.

He had been so scared. The police asked a lot of questions about the break-in at the biology lab, and it didn't take them long to start focusing on Steve. They had him at the station, asking questions, when one big cop came in with a search warrant.

They took him along when they went to search his house. Steve was sweating bullets by the time they got there, and his hands were shaking so hard one of the cops had to take the key and unlock his front door for him.

He could hardly believe it when they searched the whole house and found nothing. Zero. Zip. They had brought dogs along, too, looking for dope. They didn't find any, though. He wasn't *that* stupid.

He had never asked Nick what became of all those boxes of electronic gear. Some of his tools had vanished, too, but Steve figured that was only fair. He didn't expect Nick to work for nothing.

Now he shows up full of advice. Maybe Steve should take him up on some of it, at least the part about the girl. Nick ought to know about girls. He's what they call a chick magnet, with his movie-star looks and his slick style.

Steve scratched lazily and yawned. The girl's folks hadn't liked him much, especially after his close call with that burglary charge. But maybe they had mellowed. Maybe Nick was right and a different girlfriend would get his mother off his back. He'd give Saundra a call.

Chapter

8

Saturday morning sparkled. The rains left a washed earth that glistened with thousands of sun-generated diamonds. Marissa looked out of the kitchen window. Blue-jeans-and-sweatshirt weather. She felt more like herself this morning than she had all week. She pulled on her clothes and gave her curls a quick brush before she hurried out to meet the day. The shop door was slightly open. Uncle Paul must already be at work.

A van pulled off the highway and turned under the arch toward the parking lot. Its doors burst open almost before it stopped rolling, and a flood of children gushed out. Marissa hurried toward the carousel.

The morning passed in a flurry of band-organ music and smiles. Every time the parking lot emptied a little, another surge of tourists arrived. Some sat at the picnic tables and ate hot dogs from the Snack Shack. Parents leaned against the railing to watch the children ride. The ones with cameras called out their kids' names, hoping to capture a wave or smile

41

in a photograph. Some smiled at Marissa as she checked to be sure the leather belt loops were snug or lifted a little one down at the end of the ride.

They didn't seem to notice, or care, that she was awkward. She had learned to move on and off the platform using the brass poles for support. She always started with what Uncle Paul called the king horse, and moved around the circle supporting herself with a hand on an animal's neck or rump. When she reached the king horse again, she knew she had checked the whole circle, and she swung down to the control box. Then she pushed the start button and leaned against the fence to enjoy the riders' reactions.

She saw every kind of attitude: confident, excited, dreamy, afraid. Some faces revealed the delicious thrill of being a bit scared, knowing all the while that there was no actual danger. Marissa understood that temptation to flirt with danger. She also understood the need to feel safe.

Happy voices embroidered the music. Marissa added another kind of laughter to her list, one she knew existed but sometimes forgot. It was Joyful.

Lots of the adults rode with their children, but Marissa especially enjoyed watching the adults who rode alone. She was sorry for the ones who obviously yearned to ride but didn't. Maybe they thought it was a foolish thing for a grownup to do. She hoped she would never be that grown-up.

She let herself be carried along in the rhythm of the carousel. Each time it emptied, she opened the gate to let new riders board. She checked to be sure that everyone was safely mounted, then pushed the button to start the ride. Three minutes later, she made sure everyone got off safely, then started the process again. All the while, the band-organ music sang out the old tunes: "Humoresque," "The Beer Barrel Polka," and her favorite, the song she most associated with the fantasy adventure of the ride, the delicate "Carousel Waltz."

Uncle Paul came out of his shop to sell pop and candy from the Snack Shack, adding the smell of fresh popcorn to the mixture of colors and sounds that embraced the customers. Business only increased at noon.

Marissa stole a minute to call Cindy and ask her to come help in the Snack Shack so she and Uncle Paul could have a break. By midafternoon she figured that nearly two hundred people had stopped for a ride on their way to or from the coast.

Of the two hundred, only half a dozen had spoken to her as if they really noticed her. She didn't mind that. In fact, she liked it. She could pretend to be part of the machinery.

At nearly three o'clock the crowd still showed no sign of diminishing. People were taking advantage of the rare November sunshine. She stood at the gate, collecting dollar bills from hands of all sizes. A little boy who was going on his third turn grinned up at her and announced that he would ride the giraffe this time. She watched to be sure he was able to climb up to the high saddle. When she turned back she found herself staring into a face she recognized.

His black hair was as dense as a deep forest, and his eyes were as blue as the glass gems on the king horse's saddle. He held out two dollars and she accepted them without a word. He didn't show any sign that he had ever seen her before.

Why should he? She was certain that as far as he was aware, she was no more than a fixture. It didn't matter to him that she was also a person. To be fair, his attention was distracted, as before, by the girl clinging to his arm. One thing was different, though. It wasn't the same girl.

This one was blond too, but she didn't look anything like a Nordic doll. She was tall, almost as tall as he was, and her long straight hair hung down her back like the fringe on a 1920s dress. It swished from side to side as she walked, keeping time with her steps.

He let her choose her mount. She picked an elegant jumper in the inside row. With all four feet in midair, the horse seemed capable of leaping from the circle and carrying the girl away. She sat with easy grace and smiled at her companion while he snugged the leather belt around her, then climbed up onto the pig next to her horse. His eyes never left her face.

A family of five—two parents, a toddler, a preschool boy, and a bored-looking teen—were next in line. By the time everyone was safely and happily in place, Marissa had almost forgotten the couple. When she started the carousel, though, she watched the girl's happy expression. Marissa thought she looked as if she had just been elected Homecoming Queen . . . *and* won the lottery.

She wondered how it felt to be that happy. When the couple appeared from the far side of the circle, the girl was laughing with her head thrown back. Her long hair brushed against the back of the fancy saddle. The young man's expression of avid eagerness never changed.

"What a hunk!" Cindy had come up behind her. "Do you let him ride free as bait for the others?"

"No, he pays just like the rest," Marissa said, "but I think we might offer him a volume discount. It's his second time this week. Second girl, too."

"Fickle. Any guy who looks that good is bound to be a cad." She tilted her head and watched them disappear around the circle, then added, "Although it might be worth it to have someone look at you like that."

The music slowed and the animals coasted to a stop. Marissa swung herself up to the platform. She made her way around the carousel, weaving between the animals and offering help to the young children as they climbed down.

A tiny girl, about six years old, cried when she realized she would have to get off. She rushed toward her parents, who laughed and told her she could ride again some other day.

By the time Marissa cleared the carousel and was ready to let the next group in, the girl and the mysterious stranger had gone. She glanced over at the highway just as his blue car turned toward the coast.

Impatiently waiting riders needed her attention. The leather straps had come off two horses, and she couldn't find them in her brief search around the carousel. She asked Uncle Paul to get replacements; then it was time to be sure that everyone was safely mounted and start the music again.

Chapter

9

Cindy's mother had driven her out to Salmon Creek with the understanding that Marissa would bring her home. By the time the crowd dwindled, it was nearly dark. Cindy, Marissa, and Uncle Paul retreated to the warm kitchen for hot chocolate. Marissa opened the newspaper to the television section, studied it for a moment, and handed it to Cindy.

"There's a Frankenstein festival on the old-movie channel that's too good to miss. Spend the night. We'll watch it together, and I'll take you home in the morning."

Uncle Paul teased them. "Don't know what the world's comin' to with you younguns dwellin' on monsters an' such," he said in his creakiest geezer voice.

"Us younguns!" Marissa managed to sound outraged. "It was your generation that made these films."

"We made carousels, too," he retorted, and headed for his shop whistling "Mighty Lak' a Rose."

"Hurry, Cindy, we're going to miss the best part," Marissa said, and the two rushed out of the kitchen.

Marissa carried a bowl of popcorn in both hands. The only light in the living room came from the television, where Boris Karloff lurched across the screen.

"He walks like me."

Cindy, following with two cans of cola and a handful of napkins, nudged Marissa with her elbow in mock disgust. Popcorn sprayed. They picked up scattered kernels and settled side by side on the couch.

Marissa had seen the movie half a dozen times, but she watched the scene as intently as Cindy. As usual she felt herself being pulled into the bizarre logic of the monster's world.

A delicate blond child sat by a lake. She reminded Marissa of the tiny six-year-old who had enjoyed the carousel so much that afternoon. Her face filled with delight as she watched the monster stumble toward her. She didn't seem to think he looked odd or to notice his clumsy gait. She greeted him as she would any welcome playmate.

He knelt beside the tiny girl. She picked a flower, showed it to him, and threw it into the water. It rocked with the motion of the waves like a little boat. She picked a second flower and handed it to him, but he seemed bewildered. She demonstrated once again, making another flower boat. The monster hesitated, then threw his flower, too.

The water sparkled. Frankenstein's monster and the child laughed together, watching their flower boats' gentle motion.

"She isn't afraid of him at all," Cindy said. "Can't she see what he is?"

"Just wait," Marissa whispered. She knew what was going to happen, but she always wished for this innocent scene to go on and on. Her eyes never shifted from the screen.

The game continued. Child and monster laughed together as they set their pretty flower boats adrift. Then the music changed. Sonorous brass notes replaced the lively strings, and the tempo slowed. Marissa winced and saw that Cindy, too, had picked up on the music's hint at nasty things to come.

The monster picked up the child. She looked as fragile as the flowers. Her expression of pleasure turned to surprise, then alarm. She squirmed to be put down, but the monster understood their game at last. They were throwing pretty things into the water to see them float. The music's intensity peaked as he threw the girl into the lake.

She spoiled the game; she didn't float at all. Ignoring her frantic struggle, the monster turned and staggered away. The camera focused on the child's hand as she sank beneath the water's surface.

No matter how often Marissa watched the scene, she was always utterly shaken by the horror of the child's death. She wanted to believe the end could be different, in spite of the hardheaded realist inside who knew it could not.

Always, too, she wondered if the monster was truly responsible for his act. He killed the little girl, of course, but he had no intention of harming her and no understanding of what he had done.

Whether or not the monster was technically responsible, the townspeople took their revenge. They chased him with torches in a scene that Marissa thought must be required in any Frankenstein movie. They trapped him in a windmill and set the windmill on fire. She felt a familiar wrench of pity as she watched him scream and bat at the engulfing flames.

"I hate this part," she said, and touched the remote control with a decisive finger. They sat in the silent dark. Marissa felt sick.

Cindy stared at the blank screen awhile, sighed, then snapped on the light. "Let's go see what your uncle Paul is doing. I like his critters a lot better than Doctor Frankenstein's."

Marissa led the way out to the shop. The carousel lights still glowed. Smudged by November mist, bright colors blended into indistinct pastels. Beyond the carousel an overhead light revealed the parking lot. Prancer and Uncle Paul's truck stood side by side, like best friends. The shop door was partly open. They could hear Uncle Paul whistling and smell the sharp fumes of paint stripper.

"Hey, will you look at this! Look what was under all that paint." He stood behind the horse, one elbow resting on the saddle, and grinned at them. Marissa thought that grin threw off at least as much heat as the woodstove. The stripped horse, though, looked forlorn. Its bare wood was freckled with nicks and dents, one ear was missing entirely, and the eye sockets were empty.

Still, it carried an air of shabby dignity. It was easy to

believe that the old animal had soaked up years of riders' emotions: laughter, wonder, and even fear. It stood so proudly that Marissa half expected it to whinny.

Then she saw what her uncle had discovered. Crouched beneath the high-curved back of the saddle was a small fox. Its ears lay back against its head; its sharp little teeth were like miniature daggers. A bird hung lifelessly from its mouth. Marissa shuddered.

"The carving is beautiful," Cindy whispered.

"Yes, but it's also horrible," Marissa said.

Uncle Paul touched the fox gently with a soft-bristled brush. "The paint was so thick that I wasn't sure what was beneath it. I thought it might be some kind of odd cherub." He flicked his brush across the surface. "This is the most lifelike carving I've ever come across."

"Come on, Marissa, don't you really think it's wonderful?" Cindy leaned closer. The fox looked out with earnest, unseeing eyes.

"I feel sorry for the bird," Marissa said, thinking of the child in the Frankenstein movie. But she admitted to herself that the fox, like the monster, was only obeying its nature. Grudgingly she added, "I guess it is a good carving."

"It's exquisite," Cindy said. "How did the carver make the fox look so alive, and the bird look so . . . well . . . so dead?" She ran her fingers lightly over the little figure, tracing snout and ears with her eyes closed, soaking up the angles and curves. "I'd give anything to be able to carve like this."

Uncle Paul had smiled as he watched her response. He brushed his hands against his pants and answered her, his words slow and careful. "If you really want to learn carving, I can teach you. This horse needs a new ear. I'll show you some tricks, and we'll see how close you can come to copying the one it still has."

Cindy used one of the twin beds in Marissa's room. Uncle Paul had bought them hoping that Marissa would bring lots of friends home for sleep-overs. So far, Cindy had been the only one, but she stayed so often that the extra bed seemed like hers.

Marissa looked forward to the time, just before sleep, when Cindy and she lay and shared dreams and disasters across the dark space between their beds. Somehow the darkness made secrets flow, and speculation didn't seem at all silly.

"It was that little fox," Cindy said in a hushed voice. "I never realized how delicate carousel carvings could be. I guess I've seen the big animals so much, I started to take them for granted. I didn't really see them anymore."

She was silent for a moment, then said, "I wonder if Ms. Pearson would let me do my art project on carousels."

"Cindy, that's a great idea. She actually suggested that I do some kind of carousel project." The pitch of Marissa's voice rose as the notion grew. "But I'd rather do my project on film history."

It wasn't that Marissa didn't want to help Uncle Paul, and she did love the magic of the carved menagerie, but she felt she was too clumsy to be an artisan. She vacuumed the shop and was available when he needed an extra set of hands, but she was more comfortable staying out of the way of the most delicate work. She did her part by running the carousel alone when it wasn't too busy, and taking care of the house.

"You've always had a talent for art," Marissa said. "I think Uncle Paul is a little disappointed that I can't help him more, but I'll bet carving will be like breathing for you."

She sank into sleep listening to Cindy's *sotto voce* chatter about carving blades and kinds of wood. Marissa's last thoughts, though, were not about carousels, or even about sharp-toothed foxes or Frankenstein's monster. They were about dark hair and a dimpled chin and startling blue eyes— the face of the man she had begun to call, to herself, the Mysterious Stranger.

Sun brightened the kitchen window the next morning. Marissa turned up the volume of the little color television that was one of Uncle Paul's rare extravagances. He liked to watch the news while he ate, and she had picked up the habit. She waited a few minutes for Cindy to wake, then increased the volume. Finally she went into the bedroom and shook Cindy.

"Time for breakfast, Sleepy."

"Take it easy, Grumpy," Cindy replied, but she sat up and blinked at the new day. "Something smells good."

Half an hour later, they were gathered in the kitchen. The sweet aroma of warm maple syrup mingled with the buttery scent of walnut French toast. Marissa sprinkled ground nuts over the batter-dipped bread on the grill and breathed deeply as the nuts turned golden brown. Cindy and Uncle Paul had already finished three slices each. Uncle Paul ate one more before he put his fork down with a clank and stood up.

"No one is going to get anything done if we sit here all day." He sounded gruff, but Marissa noticed a bounce in his step as he led Cindy out to the shop.

Marissa took the cash box from its place beside the kitchen door, picked up a new book about Bela Lugosi, and went out to the carousel to wait for Sunday customers. She finished the first five chapters before noon and gave rides to only half a dozen people. On Sunday mornings, people were either sleeping, in church, or in a hurry. Finally she put her book down and hung the sign that read ANIMALS NAPPING! PLEASE RING BELL TO WAKE THEM. She went to check progress in the shop.

Cindy was covered with tiny wood fragments. She looked up with a dreamy expression that reminded Marissa of the little girl who had first been her friend in grade school. A smudge of sawdust decorated the bridge of her nose, and Marissa had to control an impulse to pull out a handkerchief and rub the dirt away. Wood shavings lay scattered around Cindy's feet, and she held a vaguely ear-shaped block in one hand and a small, sharp jackknife in the other. She seemed adrift in the shapes and textures of the wood.

Uncle Paul stood at his workbench with his back to the door. His movements were lively, and he was whistling "Nights of Gladness" in its proper, cheerful tempo. Having Cindy to share his love for carousels might be just what he needed.

"Want to break for lunch?"

"It can't be that late already." Cindy blinked as if she were being pulled out of a trance. "Gosh, I'd better get home."

"I'll drive you after we eat," Marissa said.

"Maybe I'll take drawing next semester," Cindy said on the way home. She pulled the blade of her knife open and flicked it shut as she spoke. Uncle Paul had said he wanted her to get comfortable with it, to get so it felt like a part of her hand. She closed the knife and slid it into her jeans pocket. "It would help me do the saddle decorations. Your uncle said he might let me restore one of his horses all by myself. I would be like an apprentice."

When Prancer stopped in front of her house, she hopped out with a cheery wave and almost ran up the walk. Marissa noticed that her head was high and her shoulders back, just as if she were thinking about Rule One.

Marissa was happy for both Cindy and Uncle Paul. For herself, too, because she wouldn't have to feel guilty about not being more involved with the restoration work. She would much rather read and watch films than endure the smell of paint stripper and the endless rubbing of sandpaper over blemished wood.

On the way back to Salmon Creek, Marissa pulled in to the Gas-and-Go station to fill Prancer's tank. It could be tricky to keep the car gassed up; it didn't have a gauge and she had to watch the miles. If the engine started to sputter, she had to kick a lever to open the reserve tank. Sometimes it was awkward, but it did work; and the peculiar arrangement was one of the reasons she loved Prancer. Like her, he was one of a kind.

She got out of the car and leaned against the front fender, waiting for the tank to fill. It wasn't really raining, but a thick mist made her glad she had pulled up under the canopy of the service station.

The warning bell clanged and the attendant hurried out. A blue sedan stopped at the pump across from Marissa, one not protected by cover. The driver stayed in his car, but he leaned forward with his hands across the top of the wheel and peered up at the threatening sky.

Marissa noticed the car first, then stole a glance inside. She wasn't surprised to recognize her Mysterious Stranger.

There was no sign of the tall blonde.

Chapter 10

He drove slowly, but never so slowly that he might attract attention to himself. He kept with the normal flow of traffic. It was easy now. The excitement had left him. He felt drained. Only when he let himself remember did his breath come short and his hair bristle. It had been so close to perfection that he was a bit afraid it had only been a fantasy.

His eyes shifted to the floor on the passenger side. The tackle box was still there, beside his collapsible fishing rod in its case. The box was closed. He wanted to leave it open so he could see inside, so he could reassure himself that it wasn't a fantasy, but he didn't dare. It was dangerous enough just having it there.

He should have left it in the trunk. What if he was stopped? What if there was an accident and the box fell open and someone saw inside?

He thought about pulling over and putting the tackle box in the trunk with his gym bag. No. He couldn't bear the idea of having it out of sight. Looking at it helped him to know that the evening's entertainment had been real.

He giggled.

Humming softly, he watched the speedometer. He was eager to get home and unpack his souvenirs. He laughed out loud. The words his mother used to sing slipped into the old tune for "The Farmer in the Dell." He hummed around the pictures that played out across his memory. He remembered hiding in snowy woods and hearing a voice . . . his mother's? . . . singing.

> Where is my dear boy-o?
> My baby's in the snow.
> If he won't come to Mama
> She will pinch his tiny toe.

The fuel gauge had dropped to nearly empty. He hadn't dared to stop for gas earlier. Someone might see and remember him. Now he was close to home. No one would think it was odd if he filled up here.

It took a long time to fill the tank. He leaned forward across his steering wheel and drummed his fingers against it. He noticed a pretty little redhead leaning on an old Volkswagen Bug. It was too bad he preferred blondes.

He peered up at the sky with satisfaction. It looked like a storm was blowing in. Heavy rain would wash out footprints and obliterate signs of digging.

He jumped when the attendant knocked on the window. A

quick look reassured him. Yes, the tackle box was closed. Sometimes when he went away in his mind, he did things. He was afraid for an instant that he had opened the box. He pushed the button to roll the window down and paid the attendant with cash. He pulled out of the Gas-and-Go slowly, passing the Volkswagen without another glance.

Chapter

11

"She said restoring a carousel horse is a wonderful project." Cindy started talking as soon as they got into the car after school.

She hadn't wasted any time. The first thing she had done on Monday morning was speak to Ms. Pearson. She repeated their conversation in the breathless voice she usually reserved for talk of cute boys.

"She said I'll be learning some practical techniques and at the same time helping to preserve an important example of American folk art. She said she's looking forward to it because *she'll* be learning about carousels, too."

Marissa had never seen Cindy so excited about anything, including cute boys.

"I guess you'll be seeing even more of me. I'll have to spend most of my Saturdays in your shop." Cindy was holding the little knife again, snapping the blade in and out.

"We'll both be glad to have you around, Cindy."

"Really?" Cindy looked sober. "Look, I don't want to horn in on your life. He's your uncle, after all, and you should have first chance at working with him."

Marissa almost laughed, but Cindy looked so serious she didn't dare. "I love the carousel and I love Uncle Paul, but I don't want carousels to be my whole life. I want to work in films, maybe even be a director someday. It'll let me off the hook to have you there."

Cindy considered this for a moment, then grinned and settled back in her seat. "I can hardly wait to get started on the painting, but that comes almost last. First I have to get the old finish off and repair cracks and replace parts—"

"It sounds like a lot of work to me."

"I guess it would be if I didn't want to do it, but this is such a great project that it feels like fun, not work."

Marissa didn't reply. She concentrated on getting Prancer out of the school parking lot without adding more dents to his fenders. Her mind had wandered to *her* new interest, the one with dark hair and blue eyes.

She listened to Cindy's chatter as she drove, and she thought that running the carousel was getting to be more like fun than work, too.

On Wednesday afternoon, Cindy rode home with Marissa. She vanished into the shop without even coming into the house for a snack. Marissa had a new book on Boris Karloff. She put on her rain jacket, then settled on a chair in the ticket booth with her book in hand and a little electric heater at her feet. She was halfway through the first chapter when a movement in the parking lot caught her eye.

The blue sedan pulled up and her Mysterious Stranger jumped out. He opened the passenger door with his right hand, a bit awkwardly, but then he bowed with a grace that was as natural as a cat's, and reached in with his left hand to help his passenger. Marissa was not at all surprised to see a blonde emerge.

He reached for his wallet as they approached Marissa, but his attention to the girl never wavered. He leaned toward her and chatted, keeping her close with his left arm around her waist.

"A dollar apiece. As usual." Marissa couldn't resist the mild gibe.

He looked at her sharply, just for an instant. The lights from the carousel made his eyes seem to glow neon blue. Then he turned to help the girl up onto the platform, and the moment was gone.

This girl wasn't at all the cheerleader type. She wore huge hoop earrings and half a dozen bracelets on each arm. Her hair was blond, like the others', but the style was unique. She had brushed it from the left side up and across and gathered it in a braid that fell over her right ear. A blue-green cap perched on top of her head with its bill turned backward. Even in the cold of November, she wore sandals. Her toenails were painted scarlet.

Marissa guessed she would choose to ride the hippocampus and couldn't help smiling when the girl went straight to it.

The bizarre horse-fish combination seemed to strike a resonant chord. The girl laughed when she first saw it, then stroked its scaled tail before she climbed up. The creature's blue-green color exactly matched her hat.

Next to the hippocampus stood the giraffe. Marissa's Mysterious Stranger fastened the leather belt around the girl, fussing with it for a flirtatious moment. Then he climbed onto the giraffe and leaned toward his date with his hand outstretched. As the music rose and the carousel started to turn, they held hands across the space between.

Marissa waited in the shelter of the ticket booth. After three minutes, the animals coasted to a stop to the last notes of "The Carousel Waltz." The Mysterious Stranger and his blonde hastened off the platform and out to his car without even glancing Marissa's way. She pulled her rain jacket close and huddled over the heater while she watched the blue sedan turn west onto the Sunset Highway.

It was after four o'clock and there were no more customers in sight. At this time on a weekday afternoon, most people were anxious to get where they were going. They didn't dawdle along the way. She hung the ANIMALS NAPPING sign on the hook above the bell. Her leg felt stiff from the damp weather, and she took her time crossing to the shop.

"How's it going?"

She had to ask twice before Cindy and Uncle Paul noticed her, and then their hellos were brief. Both their heads were bent low over a worktable. Cindy had drawn an actual-size outline of her horse, and they were arranging glass trinkets on the saddle.

"Let's use this one on the bridle," Cindy said, holding up a piece of ruby-colored glass that was faceted like a gemstone. It flashed in the light as she tipped it from side to side. She surveyed the pile of colored glass. "Darn. We only have one."

"No problem," Uncle Paul said. "We'll use that one on the romance side."

Cindy looked puzzled. "What's the romance side?"

"He means on the horse's right side," Marissa answered. "American merry-go-rounds go counterclockwise. The right side of each animal faces out, and since that's the side people see most, artists put their best decorations there. They call it the romance side."

Understanding washed over Cindy's face. "I noticed that. The horse is carved in more detail on the right than on the left. I thought the carver got tired or something."

Uncle Paul ran his hand gently across the horse and patted it on the rump. "Nope, it's just like people. The public face is just a little better-looking than the private one."

The shop was crowded. Uncle Paul had jammed tables and workbenches everywhere, and parts of carousel animals cluttered every surface. Cindy had trouble maneuvering between them. She edged over to a workbench, picked up a carved foreleg, and showed it to Marissa.

"See this broken hoof? I'm filling the cracks in the leg, then I'll carve and attach a new hoof. When the whole horse is stripped and sanded and filled and reglued, I can reassemble it. Then it will be time to paint and decorate."

"Do you really think it's worth all that work, Cindy?"

Uncle Paul was only half teasing. He wanted to hear Cindy's answer.

"Absolutely," she said.

His eyes twinkled. "Well, if you think it's absolutely worthwhile, and *you* do all the work, you should have the right to name the horse. What do you think you'll call it?"

Cindy didn't hesitate. "Her. I think she's female, and I think I'll call her Jewel." She held the glass ruby up so the light danced across it.

"Good name. We'd better plan lots of spangles on her, then, so she'll live up to it."

Uncle Paul bent over the diagram and put a row of small, flat-backed jewels along the bridle. Cindy joined him. Marissa didn't interrupt again. She knew from years of experience with Uncle Paul that he would try to be polite, but he wasn't really willing to be pulled away from his work. She left, closing the door softly behind her, and went into the house to start dinner.

Marissa flicked on the television in the kitchen to keep her company as she set the table. A local newscaster's face filled the screen.

"Police still have no clue to the whereabouts of a young woman named Saundra Steward, who vanished from the Tucker mall over a week ago."

A fork clattered to the floor, but Marissa ignored it. She sat down and listened as the newscaster continued.

"Becky Jackson, a student at Andrew Johnson High School in Portland, has been reported missing as well. Police speculate that there may be a connection between the two disappearances. If anyone has seen either of these girls in the last week, please contact your local police department."

A pair of pictures flashed across the screen. On the left was the same cheerleader pose Marissa had seen in the newspaper. On the right was a formal portrait of a second girl. She was blond, too, and wore her hair piled on top of her head in a coiled braid.

The picture changed and the announcer started to talk about a groundwater pollution problem next to a town dump. Marissa finished setting the table, but she couldn't shake a feeling that the second girl had been vaguely familiar.

She rubbed a bit of fresh oregano between her fingers, dropped it into her strawberry-vinaigrette dressing, and inhaled deeply. Just right. She chopped vegetables, still thinking about the girl. She couldn't have known her. The newscaster said she was a student at Johnson High. Marissa didn't know anyone who went there.

Chapter
12

Why did they all jabber endlessly? It was like water torture; it never let up. This one had annoyed him so much that he had been forced to shorten the ceremony. He had relished the silence when it finally came.

The constant chatter wasn't all. The slut had laughed at him. She thought he was joking when he first pulled off the highway. Come to find out, she was a tart. She thought he wanted sex, and she was apparently willing. She didn't start to panic until he brought out the leather straps.

Then she had tried to open the passenger door. She hadn't laughed much after that.

Correction. She hadn't laughed at all after that.

Other things had gone wrong, too. It had grown dark too soon and light too late. He hadn't been able to wait for sunrise, and he hated to do the Dispensation in the dark. He needed one of those battery-powered lanterns. That would leave his hands free but still let him see their eyes.

He would stop at Fix-All later in the week. He could keep

the light with his camera and other equipment, out of sight in the gym bag. He was getting pretty well equipped, like a real professional. His mind ticked off a mental list of gear: sledgehammer, ice pick, leather straps, the little specimen jars full of Formalin, and his rod and reel, in case someone snooped into his private business. He giggled. The fisherman disguise was perfect. The only question anyone asked a fisherman was "Having any luck?"

Yes indeed, thank you. He was having plenty of luck.

He glanced over at the tackle box. He had given in to the temptation to have it closer, on the passenger seat. He could reach out and pat it. If he really needed to, he could even slip the catch and open it, ever so slightly.

Rest first. He had to get to work by eleven o'clock. Most of the janitors at the university wanted two days off in a row, but he liked having Wednesday and Saturday. It gave him a couple of days between Dispensations, days he could use for the Hunt.

Mother had always warned him to pace himself. She had been right about that. He hummed softly as he drove toward town. He would get the lantern Saturday.

Chapter

13

Rain settled over the park, stealing sunlight and wrapping the Douglas fir trees like a dripping blanket. Even the carousel failed to cheer. Marissa huddled in the ticket booth for an hour in the late morning, then gave up. Saturday traffic rushed by without slowing. She listened to the windy hiss of tires on wet asphalt. No reasonable person would stop for a ride on such a soggy day.

She stretched to put the ANIMALS NAPPING sign on its hook and crossed the small grassy field to the shop. She might as well go to pick up Uncle Paul's order at the Fix-All store.

Compared to the dark day outside, the shop lights dazzled. Cindy and Uncle Paul stood under one of them. Her honey-gold hair shone like an angel's, but when she looked up her face was dirty. Her eyes danced.

"You're just in time. I finished Jewel's new hoof, and we're about to attach it."

Marissa stood close to the workbench in case they needed an extra set of hands, but she was welcome more to admire than to actually help. She did admire the carving, but she was even more impressed by their comfortable teamwork.

Cindy held up Jewel's detached leg as tenderly as if it were made of thin crystal. Uncle Paul studied it from all angles, his head tilting from one side to the other. He squinted and frowned as he applied glue with a small brush. Satisfied at last, he picked up the new hoof and carefully placed it.

"Now we'll just clamp her in place and let her cure," he said. "Hold it steady for a second."

Marissa held out a clamp. He took it from her and finally seemed to notice that there were other things in the world besides carousel animals and glue.

"Hello, Princess. Business slow out there?"

"It's raining. We haven't had a rider all morning."

"So it is." He peered at the rain-smeared window as if he had never seen it before. "We've been so busy I hadn't noticed."

"The hoof looks good," Marissa said, turning to Cindy. "You have a gift for carving."

Cindy grinned her thanks but never really took her eyes off the leg. "It's fascinating," she said in a faraway voice. "When we're done with Jewel, she'll carry riders for years. I almost feel like she's a little bit alive."

"Wait until you put her eyes in place," Marissa said. "That's when they show their own personalities."

"It's the music makes them come to life," Uncle Paul said. "The music and the other animals. They need to have company or they fade from pure loneliness. I just can't bear to see an old carousel broken up. It's like breaking up a family."

Uncle Paul had spent his life putting carousel families back together. Most had been separated because collectors would pay a lot for a single animal, thinking they were preserving American folk art. Uncle Paul thought that was like cutting the Mona Lisa into sections and selling just a nose or an ear. The real art was the whole carousel, complete with music and riders. Anything less was offensive to him, and he never hesitated to say so.

Marissa agreed, but she had heard his lecture on carousel preservation before. She hugged him and said, "I thought I'd go down to Fix-All to pick up that sandpaper. I hung up the sign, so if you two will listen for the bell, I'll go right now. I should be back in an hour or so."

"Take your time, Princess," Uncle Paul said. He was already studying Cindy's carving of Jewel's new ear, testing its position on the horse's upraised head.

In spite of the rain, Marissa enjoyed the drive to Fix-All. She felt almost weightless as she steered Prancer around graceful curves. It was like being one of those incredible ice dancers who seemed to know the secret of antigravity. In imagination, she could glide and soar. In imagination, she could dance like a ballerina, and maybe even attract the attention of Mysterious Strangers.

The lot was crowded. It looked as if the whole town had decided to spend Saturday doing home improvements. Marissa pulled her jacket hood up and ducked her head as she aimed for the door and its promised shelter. She hurried, even though she knew that hurrying emphasized her clumpy gait.

It was wet! She swerved left to avoid a puddle and collided with something soft.

"Watch out, can't you?" The voice belonged to an old woman. Wildly angry eyes glared at Marissa from beneath unruly wisps of coarse white hair. "What's wrong with you? Can't you be careful?"

Marissa muttered an apology. A hot flush of embarrassment warmed her face. She half expected the rain to sizzle against her skin. She shook the hood back so she could see better, and her red curls stirred. Rain dripped down inside her jacket.

Reaching out to steady the old woman, she repeated, "I'm really sorry."

The woman shook free. She squinted, carefully studying Marissa from the head down. Her eyes lingered on Marissa's hair, shifted to her built-up left shoe, then came slowly back up to her face. Marissa found herself holding her breath. What could be wrong?

"Don't you touch me. I don't need no trouble from no redheaded demon. You must be cursed." She turned and spat over her right shoulder, then glared at Marissa. "You stay away, hear me? You're cursed!"

Marissa jerked back. The woman's voice was low and raspy, but it might as well have been a shout. She felt her face flush hotter and glanced around to see if people had heard. No one was looking. She breathed deeply to still her voice, then muttered once more, "Sorry," and hobbled away.

She certainly didn't feel weightless anymore. Her shoulders hunched protectively and each step felt like a parody of walking. Maybe the woman was right. Maybe she was cursed. By the time she reached the front door of Fix-All, she was grateful for the rain. It disguised her tears.

The area around the service counter was so crowded that she had to take a number and wait for someone to help her. She pulled a paper tab off the roll and looked at it. Forty-four. The sign read NOW SERVING: 39. Marissa retreated to wait beside a display of lightbulbs and extension cords.

She clutched the bit of paper. At least she had a number. Sometimes in a busy crowd she was overlooked again and again. But the number meant that sooner or later it would be her turn.

Number thirty-nine wanted nails. Number forty wanted help with insulation. Forty-one had evidently given up waiting, and forty-two was there to buy a kitchen sink.

Next a clerk came up to the counter and called out, "Forty-three!"

A dark-haired man strode up to the counter and said, "I need a good electric lantern."

Marissa turned away. He wouldn't recognize her, but she still didn't want him to see her looking like a wet puppy with red-rimmed eyes.

"Forty-four!"

It was her turn. Marissa tried to edge to the left so that her back would be toward him when she reached the counter. But just as she stepped forward, the young man backed up. For the second time in ten minutes, she was nearly knocked off her

72

feet. She swayed, then steadied when he reached out and grabbed her arm.

"Sorry," he said. "Clumsy of me." He smiled at her with those blue eyes, then looked a little puzzled. "Do I know you?"

"No," she said. "You don't know me at all."

Chapter 14

He stood in the lobby of the movie theater. The next show would start in five minutes, and he was growing restless. Lots of high-school girls had come in, but they were either not his type or were with some guy. He glanced at his watch. Maybe he would have to try the music store, or maybe the Clothes Encounter. They visited those places in clusters. It was just a matter of getting one apart from her friends for a minute or two.

He smiled at himself in the mirrored wall, and then he saw her. This girl was a prize. She was beautiful and she was blond. She was with two other girls, neither of whom amounted to much. That was fine with him. He waited while they stood at the snack bar. She asked for popcorn, accepted her change, and turned. Now!

He stepped into her path and twisted his left shoulder, plowing his body into her right arm. The popcorn container bounced when it hit the floor and popcorn sprayed like water from a fountain.

A murmured apology, so quiet she had to lean toward him to hear; then he put his hand on her upper arm and looked into her face with earnest concern. By the time he had replaced her popcorn, she had given him her phone number. He hung back and watched her go into the theater with her friends just as the movie started; then he slipped in and sat in the back row.

Her hair shone in the occasional flicker of bright light from the screen. He listened to the crowd and was sure he could pick out her laughter. Just before the movie ended, he crept out. He was certain she didn't notice him following her home.

As he drove, he hummed. Now and then he formed the words, "The farmer takes a wife, the farmer takes a wife . . ."

Chapter 10

It rained all day Sunday and all day Monday, too. The slow drizzle matched Marissa's mood. She felt dreamy and a little sad. One moment she would be filled with plans for college and a career in film and maybe, in the dim future, a husband with dark hair and blue eyes. The next moment she brooded over the old woman's exclamation: "You're cursed!" It wasn't that she believed in curses. She didn't. Still, something about her had caused the woman to react that way. She was afraid it might be something she couldn't change.

She didn't talk to Cindy about her daydreams. Maybe someday she would, but for the moment they were either too private or too painful to be shared.

Cindy was so full of plans and ideas for Jewel that she didn't seem to notice Marissa's moodiness. On Tuesday afternoon she came home with Marissa and spent three hours in the shop with Uncle Paul, filling cracks and sanding surfaces.

Marissa stayed in the kitchen and listened for the occasional clamor of the carousel bell. She had decided on linguine with Tuscan tomato sauce for dinner.

"Yet another culinary triumph, Princess. You are a genuine genius with a saucepan." Uncle Paul put down his fork with a contented sigh and sat back in his chair. He reached for his mug of steaming coffee. "Girls, I have some news."

Marissa and Cindy put down their forks.

"I had a call today, from a fellow down in Eureka. He thinks he may have located two Looff horses in some guy's garage. They're in pretty bad shape, I guess, but he says I can get them dirt cheap."

"What's a Looff horse?" Cindy asked.

"Charles Looff was one of the greatest carvers of all time," Uncle Paul said. "His horses are graceful and gentle-looking. He influenced a lot of other carvers, but no one made a sweeter horse than Looff."

His eyes grew sort of dreamy. "I know another fellow back east who has five Looffs. We were sort of thinking of getting together and trying to re-create one of the old carousels." He put down his cup with a little bang. "Mind you, it'll take a lot of work, but I think we could manage it."

Cindy's face lit up. "I'll help. You know I'll help."

Uncle Paul grunted. "I'll need it. Some fool spray-painted the dang things."

Marissa knew how much he hated to see fine carvings abused. "I'll help, too. What do you want us to do?"

"Well, first of all, I need to take the pickup down to look at

77

them, then haul them home if they really are workable Looffs. That means I'll have to be gone a few days. Do you girls think you could run the carousel without me? Not during school, of course. We don't have much trade during weekdays this time of year anyway. But in the afternoons, you could watch the thing and, Cindy, you could spend the nights to keep Marissa company. What do you think?"

Cindy and Marissa both beamed.

"Great idea," Marissa said. "We'll be fine on our own, and we'll take extra-good care of the park. All we need to do is get Cindy's mom to agree."

"Mom won't mind at all," Cindy said with easy good humor. "I'll call her right now."

So it was settled. Uncle Paul would drive down the coast to California the following Sunday. It would be a day and a half's trip each way, and he would need at least a day there, so he figured he would be back just in time for Thanksgiving.

"And maybe we'll have a little extra to be thankful for," he said.

Marissa woke on Wednesday morning full of plans. She was pleased for Uncle Paul about the Looff horses, and she was absolutely delighted that he trusted her and Cindy enough to leave them in charge of the carousel. Even more important, he was leaving them in charge of themselves. The day was brimming with promise.

That afternoon at the pool, Gloria approached Marissa. "The Student Council is planning another dance after Friday's playoff game. Are you coming?"

Marissa tried to think of a way to tell her that she and Cindy wouldn't be attending any more dances. "I'm going to be busy every Friday night for the rest of my life" sounded too harsh. Besides, anyone would know it was a lie. She was never busy, any night, ever.

Gloria didn't deserve sarcasm. Marissa settled for "I don't know yet."

"Some of the freshmen need to do some growing up," Gloria offered. She didn't directly mention the Rating Game, but it was an apology. Then she lowered her voice to a confidential tone. "Listen. We make money on the dances, but we can do lots of other things, too. I have a great idea for a spring fund-raiser. The whole class could have a picnic out at your carousel park. We could have a cover charge and offer unlimited rides."

Marissa wanted to say no, but she couldn't come up with a reason that didn't sound surly. "I'll talk to my uncle."

"I still think you should run for Student Council next semester," Gloria said as she held the locker-room door open. "We need someone with your spirit, someone who can think for herself."

"I guess I could count on the sympathy vote." Marissa intended to tease, but the words sounded sullen and self-pitying. She regretted them.

Gloria replied quietly but with force. "Marissa, people don't feel sorry for you. If they ignore you, it's because sometimes you act so timid that no one realizes how much you have to offer. You're always going out of your way to help people, but you do it without a fuss. You're just what we need.

You're smart, and you're one of the prettiest girls in our class."

She opened her locker and handed Marissa the tape of *Nosferatu*. "Like this video. It was really thoughtful of you to lend it to me. You do stuff like that all the time, and you don't even realize how generous you are. It's just natural with you."

Marissa grabbed at the chance to change the subject. "Did you like it?"

Gloria grinned. "Well, I don't know if I exactly *liked* it. It was sure creepy! Mrs. Simon gave me an A on the report, though." Then she added, "Seriously, I think you should run. We need you."

"I'll think about it," Marissa said as she rubbed her hair with a towel. "But running isn't my greatest talent."

This time it was a real joke, and Gloria knew it. She was thinking up a smart answer when excited shouts interrupted them. A mob of girls descended on Gloria like ducks on a bag of bread crumbs.

"Tell us about him," one demanded.

"Is he cute?"

"What does he drive?"

"How old is he?"

Gloria's wholehearted laughter rose above the fluttering questions and comments. Marissa moved to the edge of the crowd and listened. The girls' heads bent toward Gloria, a sea of brown shades with Gloria's bright blond in the center.

"Do your parents like him?" someone asked.

"They haven't met him yet. He wants to wait until we know each other better before he faces them."

As Marissa headed for the shower, Gloria shouted after her, "I'll call you tonight."

Marissa would have to find a graceful way to say no to the Student Council and to the spring fund-raiser.

That night, she mentioned the plan to Uncle Paul and was dismayed when he said, "Great! Maybe I'll have those Looff horses restored by then, and Cindy can show off her work on Jewel."

Marissa swallowed her objections. After all, it would bring some publicity for the park. And if she ran the carousel, no one would notice her. She resigned herself to tell Gloria yes, but Gloria never called.

Marissa was puzzled when she didn't see Gloria Thursday morning. It wasn't like her to miss school. Marissa was drying herself after her swim that afternoon when Ramona came up to her. She looked sick.

"Have you heard the news? Now Gloria is missing."

Rumors flew around Pierce High like frantic birds. Gloria had run away. She had been kidnapped. She had eloped. She was pregnant and had to go out of town for an abortion.

"Maybe she was abducted by Martians," Cindy said in the car on the way home from school. "Maybe she's looking down on us from a spaceship at this very minute." She sighed. "Not funny. I know. I always figured Gloria had the perfect life. I just can't believe anything bad could happen to her."

"It's just been one day," Marissa said. "Maybe there was some misunderstanding. Maybe she had an argument with her folks and she took off for a while."

She spoke the words confidently, but she couldn't actually imagine Gloria having a serious argument with her parents, much less running away.

The mood of the whole school was glum on Friday. No news of Gloria had surfaced. The Tornadoes were facing the Tillamook Cheesemakers in the playoff game that night, and no one even bothered to make jokes. Marissa and Cindy got through the day, but neither of them intended to go to the game, much less the dance afterward.

Marissa watched the local news while she prepared Sloppy Joes for dinner that night. The community was slowly coming to the realization that *four* girls had vanished. One or two might be runaways or coincidence. Three hinted at disaster. Four missing girls shouted catastrophe.

The search for Gloria was turning desperate. The announcer looked directly into the camera lens. "If anyone has any information about what might have happened to Gloria Josephson, or if you have seen her, or think you might have seen her, please call this number. The search center hotline is open twenty-four hours a day."

The segment closed with a plea from Gloria's family. Her father was barely recognizable. There was no trace of the cheerful man who loved pizza, loved kids, and most of all loved serving pizza to kids. In his place stood an old man, bent and red-eyed. He grasped the hand of Gloria's mother and stammered a plea for his daughter's safe return. Gloria's grandmother wept.

Marissa sank heavily onto a chair beside the kitchen table and studied the faces of the grieving family. Her chest ached.

She slid her crossed arms forward across the table and rested her forehead on them. She willed tears to come, but her eyes stayed hot and dry. The thumb of her right hand moved, on its own, to rub her mother's ring, but even that brought no comfort.

Gloria couldn't be in trouble. She had sounded fine on Wednesday afternoon. She had been excited about the Student Council's plans, and about her new boyfriend.

Thinking of the boyfriend brought Marissa's mind back to her own Mysterious Stranger. She had half expected to see him at the carousel with a new girl on Wednesday afternoon, but he had not shown up. Of course it had been raining. She thought, with a slightly bitter twist, that it must have been the rain. He couldn't possibly be running out of blondes.

Saturday morning suited Marissa's mood. Rain never actually fell from the dull gray sky, but a lingering threat seeped into every breath she took. She couldn't shake a sense of disaster.

Only a few travelers stopped in the morning. She didn't need to disturb Cindy and Uncle Paul at their work in the shop. Marissa ran the carousel and sold an occasional candy bar or drink from the Snack Shack.

Just after noon, sunlight pushed through the mist, driving it up and away and replacing it with welcome brightness. Still, the rising mist failed to pull Marissa's spirits up. She had been fighting sadness ever since that awful old woman had called her cursed, and she had struggled with an awful sense of dread with every hour that Gloria wasn't found. Cindy's good cheer only made her feel more empty.

"I need a passion of my own," she muttered to the animals on the deserted carousel. "I need something to really care about."

As if in response, the blue sedan pulled into the parking lot. Marissa watched from the ticket booth, interested to see what this week's blonde would look like.

She was a little plump, but her curves were spectacular. She had extravagant curls that shook with each step.

That's not all that shakes, Marissa thought. This girl is equipped for life.

Marissa got off her stool. She was stiff from sitting so long in the damp cold. She tried to scold her left leg into behaving, but it swung awkwardly. She caught a glimpse of herself in the carousel mirrors.

No wonder the old woman had said she was cursed. She rolled like one of those weighted toys that rocks in wild circles when you hit it. The red highlights in her hair flared, her fair skin looked as pasty as a blood-starved vampire's. She looked spooky, even to herself.

She felt her hurt and frustration rise, and she steered them into anger with the ease of long practice. To heck with them all. Marissa lifted her chin and took the stranger's two dollar bills, invoking Rule One with emphasis. She was tired of looking at her feet.

He didn't notice her and neither did the girl. They replayed the scene he had acted in so often. The major difference was that this girl picked the ostrich. Marissa had to admit that its pink feathery softness matched hers. People were uncanny in their ability to choose the most suitable animal.

After their ride, the girl tugged her date's arm and pointed to the Snack Shack. Marissa followed them, not bothering to try to hide her limp.

"What can I get for you?" she asked so loudly that she startled herself. No use overdoing it, she thought, and made a note to tone down her voice. Her eyes stayed bright and confronted them levelly. Rule One.

The girl giggled and held his arm with both hands. She whispered something to him, and he turned to Marissa.

"I guess she'll have root beer and a bag of popcorn," he said. Then he tilted his head and regarded Marissa through slightly narrowed eyes. "I've bumped into you before, haven't I?"

"At Fix-All," Marissa managed. "I think *I* bumped into you."

"No matter. It's nice to see you again."

The girl glared at Marissa and gave him another tug. He paid for the drink and popcorn and they started toward the parking lot, holding hands. He didn't look back, but the girl shot a single triumphant glance Marissa's way.

Marissa had to smile. She didn't blame the girl at all.

Chapter

16

The girl last week had class. She could have been the best of them all, except for the Courtship. When he started to pull into the merry-go-round park, she said she knew the people who ran it. He had to think fast to find a reason not to go in.

Gloria. That was her name. Gloria had been glorious. She had a glorious nose. She had glorious toes. He giggled softly. It had been almost perfect. Almost.

Rituals had to be whole. An abbreviated ritual could be much worse than no ritual at all. Gloria had forced him to miss a step. He reviewed it in his mind: Hunt, Courtship, Dispensation, and Consummation. She had made him miss the Courtship ride, and he had been forced to punish her for that.

He smiled at the girl beside him, shaking his head gently to refuse the popcorn she offered. This one giggled, but she didn't jabber. Maybe this one would be perfect.

Chapter

17

Marissa watched the last car leave the lot. She turned the red-tagged key to shut down the carousel and lifted the cash box out of its drawer. It was time to start dinner. Cindy would eat with them again tonight.

"It's the very least we can do, considering all the labor you're donating," Uncle Paul had declared to Cindy.

She had just laughed at him and said it was play, not work. "But I'll eat Marissa's cooking *almost* anytime."

Marissa knew that the "almost" referred to a disastrous dish involving tofu and pineapples. She had actually enjoyed throwing that one in the disposal.

She thought Uncle Paul seemed younger now that he had someone to play with. He and Cindy were as enthusiastic as little kids, turning beaten-up hunks of wood into vibrant creatures born of imagination and elbow grease.

Marissa had a new recipe for Greek stuffed eggplant with béchamel sauce. The recipe demanded that she stir the flour and butter together "for several minutes." The wire whisk made a brisk, rhythmic sound against her stainless-steel pot. Her hands were busy, but her mind was free, and it went immediately to her favorite subject.

He was heart-wrenchingly handsome. But Cindy was right —he was obviously a cad. That wasn't necessarily such a bad thing, though. It could actually be an advantage for her. Marissa knew about all the girls, but each of his darling blondes seemed to believe she was his one true love. He was certainly a master at convincing them of it.

Well, why shouldn't he be? There was no law against having lots of girlfriends, and he obviously made each one happy, at least for a little while. He was nice to them. There could be no harm in that.

Being so outrageously handsome didn't hurt, either. She let her mind drift through a catalog of his obvious gifts: the dimple, his hair and eyes, the tender, eager way he concentrated on each girl in turn.

Marissa wouldn't mind having him look at her that way, even knowing that it was just for a short while. In fact, knowing that would protect her. It would keep her from being hurt when he moved on to the next girl.

There was a chance, too, that if he found the right girl, he wouldn't move on. She let herself fantasize about being enough for him, enough to make him forget the other girls and her ugly leg. She knew it was fantasy, but it gave her comfort. Even a hardheaded realist had to dream sometimes. Maybe it didn't have to be only a dream. If she couldn't outrun the other girls, just maybe she could outsmart them.

Marissa looked at her reflection in the kitchen window. Her

sandy red hair could be intriguing, with its softness and sudden flashes of color. Her cluster of curls shimmied when she shook her head. Her liquid green eyes were definitely her best feature. She decided she needed a touch of drama to emphasize her strong points. She needed something that would pull his attention up, away from her leg.

She added just a bit of salt and a single grinding of white pepper to the sauce and tasted it. Perfect.

After dinner, Uncle Paul packed for his trip and Cindy helped with the dishes. Then Marissa drove her home.

"He was here again this afternoon."

"Who? The guy with the macho complex?"

"That's not fair! He's nice." Marissa hadn't meant to defend him so vigorously, but Cindy's attack had been instantaneous. She had just responded.

"Who was he with this time?" Cindy was unrepentant.

"Another blonde. She was the jealous type."

"I don't blame her. She has a lot to be jealous of."

Marissa could see this was going to be a dead end. Cindy wouldn't even give him a chance.

"You've judged him and you don't even know him."

Cindy didn't hesitate. "Absolutely," she said with conviction. "The guy's a beast."

Chapter

18

"Goodbye, Princess. Are you sure you'll be all right?"

"That's the manymillionth time you've asked," Marissa said. "Are you looking for a reason to stay home?"

"No." He gave her a lingering hug and climbed up into the pickup's cab. "You and Cindy be good, now. Don't throw any wild parties while I'm gone. We geezers know how you teenagers can be." He grinned down at her with something close to pure joy. "See ya later, favorite girl."

"So long, favorite guy."

"I'll call tonight. You be careful, now." He winked and put the truck into gear. A minute later he was out of sight, down the road toward the coast.

"You too," Marissa whispered as she watched him go. Something gentle fluttered inside her. She identified a tiny bit of loneliness and a lot of excitement. This was a test she was ready for. She looked around the park. Everything was in order. All she had to do was be around to greet people and operate the carousel. Cindy's mom would bring her over in the afternoon. The sun was even shining. What could be better?

She had an idea. Back inside the house, she rummaged through her closet until she found what she needed: the sea-green sweater Uncle Paul had given her last Christmas. She hadn't worn it much, thinking it was too good for every day. She tried it on and was pleased that it fit better than ever.

Gloria's green ribbon lay on the dresser. Seeing it, Marissa felt a twinge of fear for her friend. Thinking that wearing it would make Gloria feel closer, she wrapped it around her head and tied it, trying for a duplicate of the pretty bow Gloria had tied. Regarding the effect in the mirror, she decided it had exactly the right spirit. The only thing needed was attitude, and she vowed to provide that.

The sweater and ribbon might distract someone from looking at the rest of her too carefully. Gloria had said she was pretty, but Marissa wasn't used to that idea. The mirror over her dresser reassured her. She was at least all right, and maybe even a little more than all right. It didn't matter anyway. She had nothing to lose. At least she wouldn't be invisible.

Sunday afternoon, business was brisk. Even in late November, sunshine brought out the tourists. Cindy arrived at noon to help in the Snack Shack. If she noticed Marissa's new look, she didn't comment.

Things slowed down at about four o'clock. It would be dark in just over an hour, and people were hurrying to get home. Cindy went into the shop to work on Jewel. Marissa turned off the carousel, put the key ring on the counter, and was hanging the ANIMALS NAPPING sign when she saw the blue sedan. She looked toward the passenger side, wondering what this blonde would be like.

He was alone.

Marissa retreated behind the counter of the ticket booth. She hadn't expected to see him on a Sunday, but she was glad she had worn the green sweater. She quickly checked her image in a mirror. It would have to do. She felt confident as long as he could only see her from the waist up. She leaned forward and smiled, trying for Interesting.

"Hello, Sunshine," he said. He glanced at the carousel, then fastened his blue eyes on Marissa's face. "I see you have something that's going around."

It was corny, but at least it was a place to start. "It's like life. What goes around comes around."

His steady gaze flickered. "I've never understood what that means, exactly," he said.

Marissa laughed. "You caught me. Neither do I."

Then, partly to tease and partly to let him know she wasn't a fool, she said, "Where's your friend . . . or should I say, where are your friends?"

He laughed. "Now *you* caught *me*. I'm all alone." His face turned serious, almost soulful. "I'm alone a lot of the time. I could use a friend, really."

Marissa felt a little flash of rage. Did he think she was that needy? Did he think such a simple ploy was all she was worth?

He must have noticed her anger, because he ducked his head and smiled, nodding slowly. "Everyone needs friends, right? I'm no different from anyone else."

His hair really was the rich black of a raven's wing. She studied it, noticing its texture and the soft curls that nestled around his ears. She fought an entirely insane urge to stroke the place where his hair lay against his neck. She hoped desperately that someone would drive up and want a ride; she hoped desperately that no one would drive up and want a ride.

He straightened and grinned at her with the open face of a child. He shrugged, holding his arms out, palm up, as if to show that he had nothing to hide.

"Maybe it's time for me to get to know a redhead," he said softly. "How about it? Can you go to a movie with me tonight?"

Marissa felt like a struck bell. He was asking her on a date, a real date, with movies and maybe popcorn and conversation and . . . she wasn't sure what else. She hadn't let herself hope for even this much.

Her chest felt tight. The timing couldn't be worse. Her voice shook a little when she answered. "I can't tonight. My uncle is away and I have to be here when he calls." Then, in case that sounded as if she were just a child who had to be checked on, "He worries a lot."

"Some other time, then," he said easily. "I'd like to see you again."

He stayed and chatted for a few more minutes; then, almost abruptly, he turned and walked away. Marissa had spent the whole time behind the counter, and she didn't offer to walk with him.

He waved a salute before he opened the car door. She waved back, suddenly realizing that she didn't know his name and he had not asked hers.

"Some other time," she murmured to herself, and felt a thrill she identified as Hope.

Chapter 19

He pulled carefully out onto the coast highway, headed east toward Portland. His fury shook him so deeply that he could hardly breathe, but his body remained still. Finally, when he was sure he was out of sight of the Salmon Creek Park, he threw back his head and screamed. The muscles in his neck and jaws tensed and rippled, and he beat his fists against the steering wheel as he roared.

She knew. She had seen him with each one of them, except the one called Gloria. She wasn't stupid. He had made a serious mistake. He knew better than to make mistakes. His mother had taught him that, plenty of times.

All his achievements, all the painstaking effort, now depended on his ability to deal with that pitiful little bitch.

His rage spent, he gulped in air and reached over to pat the tackle box on the seat beside him. His hand slid down and caressed the set of keys. The slut hadn't even noticed when he slid them off the counter and put them in his pocket.

He drove east carefully. He still had to rest before he went to work, and he thought it was time to make a phone call to the police.

Steam rose from the cup of hot chocolate Marissa cradled in her hands. She and Cindy sat at the kitchen table with a plate of double-chocolate brownies between them. They had hurried home after school to turn on the carousel lights, and now they were relaxing while they watched for customers.

"You're so moony, I'd swear you were in love." Cindy was using colored pencils to sketch carousel horses in different poses. She reached for a brownie and took a bite, rolling her eyes in mock ecstasy. "Ummm."

"I'm just thinking about Uncle Paul. I hope the horses are real Looffs."

It wasn't the whole truth, though. Mixed in with her thoughts of Uncle Paul was the recurring image of blue eyes, and of dark hair lying against the curve of a neck. He had seemed so vulnerable. She felt an odd, dizzying tenderness. Cindy was right. She was moony.

She wanted to share the feeling, but she was afraid to. Cindy might make a joke of it. Worse, Cindy might be right about him. He might be playing some crueler version of the Rating Game.

It was irrelevant anyway. She might as well enjoy being a little moony. She didn't really expect him to come back for a girl with a twisted leg, not when he could have any other girl, anytime he wanted.

Marissa held the cup of chocolate under her nose and took a deep breath, pulling in the fragrance. She had used a new recipe that called for heavy cream and nutmeg. She was about to take a sip when the phone rang.

"Hi, Princess. Anything interesting happen at school today?" Uncle Paul sounded cheerful, but his voice was tinny. He seemed very far away.

"No, nothing at all."

"Nothing about locomotion in the three-toed sloth? Are they still pretending some guy actually walked on the moon?"

"Nothing of interest at all," she said, but she thought, Unless you count Mysterious Strangers.

"Is everything all right? Is Cindy there with you?"

"Everything's fine. We came right home from school and we're just sitting in the kitchen, waiting for our first customer."

She didn't mention misplacing the keys. She was certain they would show up in some stupid spot, and meanwhile she could use the spare set. "What about you?"

"I'm in Eureka. The guy with the horses won't be home from work for a couple of hours, so I won't get to see them until later. If we can make a deal, I'll try to leave tomorrow, but I may have to stay another night. Will you and Cindy be all right for an extra day?"

"Sure we will. You'll be home by Thursday, won't you? Cindy's mom has invited us for Thanksgiving dinner."

"Great. I'll try to get there late Wednesday, but it might be closer to turkey time on Thursday. I'll be there, though. I've tasted that lady's pumpkin pie. It's almost as fine as yours."

His voice was almost too cheerful, but the little silence that followed told Marissa more than his words. She responded to the silence. "Uncle Paul, take good care of yourself and please don't worry so much about us."

"Can't help it, Princess. We geezers use worry as a form of entertainment."

Marissa laughed. "So do we younguns. Good luck with the Looffs."

Tuesday was a repeat of Monday. Speculation about Gloria had exhausted itself. People waited silently for news. Marissa and Cindy talked about everything but Gloria on the way home in Prancer. There were only a half dozen riders for the carousel that afternoon, and they ate an early dinner of autumn vegetable soup and oven-warm country cornbread. Marissa sat across from Cindy and flicked on the television with the remote control.

"Light showers will persist through the early part of the week, and there is a good chance of rain on Thanksgiving Day, with some snow at higher elevations." The weather-woman's voice droned through the highs and lows.

After dinner, Cindy went out to the shop to work on Jewel. The phone rang just as the door closed behind her.

Uncle Paul sounded thrilled. "This fellow says he thinks he knows where we can find a Looff camel. I think it's worth a look, but it means I'll have to detour through Roseburg on my way home. Can you girls hold the fort through Thursday morning? If I leave early tomorrow, I think I can make it home just in time for Thanksgiving dinner."

His voice sounded like a kid's. Marissa smiled and said, "Sure. Take your time. If you're late, we'll save you some pumpkin pie." She was still smiling when she hung up. Then she noticed the picture on the television. She gasped and nearly dropped the phone.

A photograph of a pretty blond girl filled the screen. She had curls and a round face with deep dimples. It was the girl who had been with her Mysterious Stranger last Saturday.

The kitchen faded from her awareness. Marissa's whole world filled with the television image and the announcer's voice.

"This is the latest in a series of disappearances. Gloria Josephson vanished from her home last Wednesday, and three other girls, Trish Hanson, Becky Jackson, and Saundra Steward, have also been reported missing."

Pictures of each girl flashed on and off the screen in sequence. Marissa was afraid she would throw up. Her Stranger had been with each of them except Gloria, or at least he had been with girls who looked like them. She had to tell someone.

She picked up the telephone, thinking she would call the

police, when another picture appeared. This one was of a young man with a hesitant smile and mussed hair. The announcer continued.

"In a major breakthrough, Steve Parker has been arrested at his home in southeast Portland. Parker dated Saundra Steward briefly last spring. Police say they received an anonymous tip that caused them to take a closer look at him. They discovered convincing physical evidence of his involvement in this troubling case. Mr. Parker was previously investigated in connection with a burglary at Portland Metropolitan University. Neighbors describe him as quiet, a loner who often comes and goes at odd hours of the day and night. His mother was interviewed earlier today."

The screen showed a middle-aged woman with hair the same color as her son's and red-rimmed, mascara-smudged eyes. "This is preposterous," she said. "My son has never been in trouble. He's a good boy. Ask anyone." She wiped her eyes with the back of her hand, smearing her mascara further, and sniffed wetly.

Marissa put down the phone.

That night she stayed awake long after Cindy had given up trying to engage her in their usual presleep confidences. Cindy's steady breathing contrasted with Marissa's turmoil. She couldn't deny the cold fact that she had seen her Mysterious Stranger with four of the missing girls.

Or could she? They did look like the girls she had seen, but there was no way to be absolutely certain they were the same. It could be coincidence, or her memory could be faulty. After all, she had looked mostly at him, not at his dates.

Marissa was absolutely certain of one thing. She had never seen him with Gloria.

Anyway, she just couldn't convince herself that he would hurt those girls. She had seen the way he fussed over them. No one could have been more attentive. He might be fickle, but each girl had felt the full force of his passionate interest. She couldn't imagine her Mysterious Stranger doing anything truly harmful. He had been so caring, and his eyes had been so full of tenderness. His voice had been soft and deep, with a comforting tone she had never heard from any boy she knew. Of course, he wasn't a boy. He was a man. The maturity showed in everything he did, and that was part of his appeal. He wasn't a juvenile jerk.

Marissa remembered the vulnerable way he had looked at her, and with the memory came an image of the hair curling across his exposed neck. All the years of being brutally honest with herself forced her to admit that she didn't want her suspicions to be true.

He had been open with her; he had said he needed a friend. She certainly knew how that felt! Maybe she could get him talking and ask if he knew Gloria. She would probably never even see him again, but if she did she would give him a chance to explain. Everyone deserved that.

After all, there was no evidence that any of the girls had actually been harmed. They were just missing.

She could almost hear what Uncle Paul would say. "That's cold comfort."

Marissa smiled to herself in the dark. It was a phrase a little like "what goes around comes around." She thought she knew what it meant, but couldn't put it in any better words.

There was no actual evidence that the missing girls had been forced away from home, or even that they had been hurt. True, it was out of character for Gloria to go off and not tell her folks, but Marissa had no way of knowing about the other girls. Maybe they had just run away.

Most important, someone had already been arrested. The police sounded pretty confident that they had the right person.

What had she really seen, anyway? Only that someone whose name she didn't know had been with a few girls who looked a little like the pictures of the girls who were missing. It sounded pretty lame. The police would think she was a pitiful teenager longing for attention. Sure, she would tell someone, but first she would find out a little more.

Like his name, for heaven's sake, she thought. I'm such a dummy I'm still calling him a Mysterious Stranger. She vowed that if he came back she would find out his name and get his car's license-plate number. Then she could report everything she had seen, or imagined, and it would be out of her hands.

Sleep finally came after midnight.

On Wednesday morning, Pierce High buzzed with news of the arrest. People were more afraid than ever about what might have happened to Gloria.

"I hear he was a student at the college," someone said.

"They found body parts at his house," another whispered,

pronouncing the awful words carefully, as if tasting their horror.

Ramona was at the center of a silent circle of girls. They looked numb.

Even the teachers seemed just to be going through the motions of a normal school day. The routine of classes and daily schedules served as an anchor, holding them all in place.

That evening, Cindy and Marissa ate fast food. "I just didn't feel like cooking," Marissa said.

"Wow, that's a first," Cindy replied. She unwrapped her hamburger, took a bite, then put it down. "Actually, I'm not very hungry anyway." With a wry smile, she added, "I guess that's another first."

Marissa had hoped she would see her Mysterious Stranger, but he hadn't shown up that afternoon. She had come to assume that Wednesday was one of his usual days. Maybe he had come earlier while they were at school, or more likely he wouldn't come back because he was afraid that she expected something from him. He might think she would make a scene if he brought another girl to the park. He probably regretted having spoken to her.

The plan for Thursday was that Cindy would watch the carousel in the morning. People would be traveling, and some of them would want to stop for a ride. Marissa would make her sweet potato surprise with apples and fresh ginger to take for Thanksgiving dinner at Cindy's house. She knew that Uncle Paul wouldn't think it was Thanksgiving without his sweet potato surprise.

They went to bed early. Marissa thought sleep would be hard, but she drifted off right away.

She awoke to the faint sound of carousel music. The clock said one-thirty. Uncle Paul must have got home early and couldn't wait to show them his new treasures.

She glanced across the room. Cindy lay, as usual, buried in blankets and oblivious to any movement or sound.

Marissa swung herself out of bed. The cold floor stung her bare feet. Without her lift, her body jerked each time she put her left foot down. She held on to the edge of the window and peered out. Uncle Paul's truck was nowhere in sight, but a blue sedan stood beside Prancer under the parking-lot light.

Carousel lights glowed diffusely through the mist. The animals rose and fell as they trod their familiar circle. The beat of drums and clang of cymbals set a steady rhythm while bells tinkled out an incongruous tune: "The Beer Barrel Polka."

Chapter

21

Marissa pulled on jeans and her green sweater. The chair in the corner was heaped with clothes, so she sat on her bed to put on her custom-made sneakers. She kept an eye on Cindy, watching the steady rise and fall of her blanket as she slept. Cindy's mother had once said army maneuvers through the bedroom wouldn't wake her. Marissa moved silently. She was adult enough to handle this on her own.

She grabbed a pencil and a little message pad and went back to the window. She stood behind the curtain, pulling it back just enough so she could see out without being observed. Maybe she could make out the sedan's license number. No, she was too far away. Then she saw him. He was in the shadow of the ticket booth, watching the house.

Marissa thought ruefully, This is hardly the way I imagined my first date. The green ribbon Gloria had given her stuck out of the tangled pile of clothing. On an impulse, she tugged it free. Cindy's little knife clattered on the floor, and Marissa slipped it into her own pocket. Then, with a glance to be certain that Cindy was still asleep, she went into the bathroom. She ran a brush through her curls, wound the ribbon around her head, and tied a little bow. She slid her arms into her forest-green rain jacket and slipped the pad and pencil into a pocket. She silently stepped out into the night.

The carousel coasted to a stop as she crossed the yard. She moved slowly. He had come; he would wait. She kept Rule One in mind and held her head high.

He had no way to know that Marissa connected him with the missing girls. She would talk to him and give him his chance to explain.

As she came up beside the ticket booth she called out, "So you're the one who took the keys. I thought I had lost them."

He stepped in front of her, swift and silent as a wraith. Even having expected him, she started.

"I hoped you'd come out alone," he said.

"No need to wake anyone else," she answered. Best to let him think that Uncle Paul is back, she thought.

"Good. It's you I came to see."

"In the middle of the night?" Marissa managed to sound just annoyed enough to keep him on the defensive.

He ducked his head and lowered his eyes, then looked at her from beneath thick lashes. He reminded her of an apologetic cocker spaniel, whose mischief wasn't really so bad as to deserve harsh words. She almost felt guilty.

"It's my night off," he said softly. "I work the graveyard shift, so this feels like daytime to me." He glanced at his watch. "One-thirty. The day is just beginning. I know it's late for you, but I was wide awake and couldn't stop thinking about you. I came out here hoping you would ride with me." His voice was velvet. He pointed to the keys now hanging from the carousel's control panel. "You don't mind, do you? I borrowed them last Sunday."

It was harder to keep the cool tone in her voice. "As a matter of fact, I do mind. I searched everywhere for them."

He looked so crestfallen that Marissa hastened to add, "I was afraid someone had stolen them." She tried not to press too hard. She didn't want him to think she was accusing him. "Since you had them, I guess it's okay."

He brightened a bit and gestured toward the carousel. "I was thinking about you and wondering which one is your favorite animal."

Marissa was happy to change the subject. "I guess if I had to choose, I'd pick the hippocampus. But I like them all."

He leaned close, slipping his arm around her waist. "Which is your favorite right now?"

She knew he was asking about something other than carousel figures. She even knew that it was dreadfully corny, almost comical. Still, his face was close, his lips were curved into a gentle smile, and his eyes were fastened on her face as if his whole future depended on her answer. The little curls still curved around his neck in delicate wisps.

Marissa placed her palm against his chest and gently pushed him away. "I think we need to talk. I need to ask you if you know a friend of mine."

He shifted the subject once more. "Let's turn it on again and ride," he suggested.

"It's late," she said, thinking of Cindy. She didn't want to wake her, especially now. "I'll turn the music off and then we'll ride."

She rotated the volume dial counterclockwise as far as it would go, then pressed the start button. It felt unfamiliar under her finger, as if she were pushing it for the first time. The bell shrilled briefly and the platform creaked as it broke free of stillness and started to turn.

She grabbed a brass pole and swung herself easily up onto the moving platform. She had had lots of practice. Steadying herself by a hand on the neck of each animal as she passed it, she walked forward toward the Philadelphia Toboggan Company sleigh, which Uncle Paul sometimes called the lovers' tub. They could sit side by side and talk as they rode.

He followed. He staggered slightly, fighting for balance on the moving floor. Marissa felt an unfamiliar sense of power. On her own turf, she was actually more agile than he was. She didn't turn to look at him; let him follow as best he could. She reached the lovers' tub and sat down, patting the seat beside her. He sank onto the bench with an awkward lurch that Marissa found endearing. She knew how it felt to be clumsy in front of other people.

The carousel picked up speed. In front of them the horses rose and fell and the platform shook under their feet. The lifters creaked. The animals seemed to strain.

"It's odd without the music," Marissa said. "It must be the music that makes the magic."

"I think you make the magic," he whispered.

Marissa almost laughed before she realized he wasn't joking. She had never heard anyone talk like that, at least not outside of soppy old movies. It took a little effort to arrange her expression so he wouldn't think she was mocking him, but she couldn't answer as though she took him seriously.

"You say that to all the girls," she cooed, sounding every bit as stupid as she felt.

"Ah, but this time I mean it," he countered. He picked up her hand, casually wrapping his fingers around hers. He was so warm! She hadn't been ready for this. He probably wouldn't believe it if she told him he was the first man ever to touch her, even in this innocent way. She felt a little giddy, but she blundered on.

"I need to ask about my friend. Her name is Gloria."

He regarded her with an entirely serious expression, as if he wanted to soak up every word. Marissa talked faster.

"A number of girls have disappeared in the last few weeks, and my friend is one of them. I'm scared that she might be in trouble. I just wondered if you knew her . . . or anything about her."

He stroked the top of her hand, and his eyebrows moved together slightly, into a frown of puzzled innocence. "I don't understand. Do you think I had something to do with her or with these other girls?"

The sky blue of his eyes clouded, and his mouth formed a brittle line. She had offended him. Silence clotted between them, and Marissa wished she had left the music on. She was so in tune with the carousel that she sensed how many turns they had gone through. This was only number four. There would be eleven more. They had slipped out of normal time somehow. Tonight, fifteen revolutions seemed to need thirty minutes, or three hundred—certainly not just three.

There were questions she had to ask. She rested her free hand on his and gazed at him soulfully. She sighed. She gazed some more, thinking of the expressions she had seen on the other girls' faces. He started to relax.

"I'm sorry," she said. "I'm very bad at this. I didn't mean to hurt you."

He turned slightly to take her hands in both of his. "It's just awkward. You've seen me with lots of girls. It's kind of embarrassing. I hope you understand, I'm not with them now. I'm with you. You're the only one who matters."

Marissa wondered if she had stepped into waters too deep. She might drown in this confusion. She was having trouble breathing. The giddy feeling created by his closeness and his words tantalized her. It would be so easy, so joyous, to give in. She yearned to follow that path as far as it would take her. Still, she knew she ought to retreat. She didn't dare believe him. She knew better than to believe him. She wanted to believe him. She needed to believe him.

She smiled down at their joined hands and whispered, "I do understand."

The moving parts of Uncle Paul's carousel screeched as they rubbed against each other. When the music played, Marissa had never noticed how the machinery creaked and groaned. Her shiny world felt tarnished; the fantasy was exposed as sham. At last the carousel shuddered to a halt.

Her Stranger squeezed her hands ever so gently, as if his

own were a breeze, not made of muscle and bone. He stood and helped Marissa from the seat, then led her off the platform.

"Thank you," he said. "That was perfect. I guess I've disturbed your sleep long enough. Will you walk me to my car?"

His hand under Marissa's left elbow steadied her as he urged her down the path to the parking lot. Then he said the words she had once hoped to hear: "You're different from the others."

Marissa dropped her chin and lowered her eyes. Let him think he had reached her heart. Part of her acknowledged that he actually had.

She felt his hand on her as heat, distracting her from what she knew she must do. She edged to the right, away from him, but his fingers closed slightly with just a little more pressure than was comfortable. She deliberately pulled her arm from his grasp. He looked surprised.

She edged away from him and stole a quick glance at the car. One more step and she could make out his license number. She didn't dare write it down with him watching, but she squeezed her eyes shut for a second, concentrating on squeezing the number into her memory. Casually, she hoped, she leaned on the car's front fender and faced him.

"I don't even know your name, and I don't think you know mine."

"I'll bet it's beautiful," he said. The parking-lot light illuminated his face from above, carving dark shadows under his eyebrows, nose, and chin. His eyes remained hidden.

"Marissa," she said.

"You see. It is beautiful." The silence held a beat too long before he added, "I'm Nick Farmer."

Marissa relaxed a little. She had a name and a license number. All she had to do now was get him talking. She desperately wanted to hear his explanation for being with those girls.

"Where do you meet so many girls, Nick?" It was a place to start.

"I don't chase them, if that's what you mean. Mostly they come on to me. That's what attracted me to you. You're shy. Sweet. You would never throw yourself at a guy."

"What do you do with them when you get tired of them?" It was a dangerous question. She held her breath, waiting for his response.

"I don't ever get tired of them. They get tired of me." His hands moved restlessly at his sides. "It's cold out here. Come sit with me." He held the passenger door open in invitation.

"Do you know my friend Gloria? She's a pretty blonde, and she goes to Pierce High. She's been missing for a week and we're all worried sick."

Nick frowned, then took a shuddering breath. He moved to stand, with his feet planted wide, between Marissa and the path back to the carousel. Shrugging broadly, he held his arms open with his palms up. "Look, they arrested some guy already, didn't they? Are you accusing me of something?"

He sounded like an innocent man, wrongly condemned. But as he raised his face toward the light, his eyes turned from sky to ice. A muscle in his cheek twitched wildly, and he clenched his open hands into fists. He took a step toward her.

Marissa wasn't fast enough. Nick closed in like a snake

striking. He pinned her arms and lifted her off her feet. She screamed once, then gagged when his hand gripped her throat. His thumb dug into her neck. She felt awful pain, then slipped into unconsciousness.

As if through thick cotton, she heard a dull metallic snap and realized it was the sound of the seat belt being fastened across her chest. His hands were hot against her skin as he wrapped a leather strap around her crossed wrists. With an animal grunt, he pulled the strap tight and buckled it. She recognized it as one of those missing from the carousel.

She kicked wildly, but in the confined space she couldn't maneuver to aim and couldn't get enough momentum to hurt him. He grabbed her feet and bound her ankles with a second strap.

She screamed. He forced her back with his elbow in her throat. She gagged and heard a faint whistling as she struggled to draw air into her lungs; then dizziness pulled her down to darkness again.

"We don't want you to get hurt in an accident," he said tenderly as he tightened the seat belt around her. "Oh no indeed. We don't want anything bad to happen to you."

He giggled.

*S*nap-snap. The doors and windows secure, he backed out of the parking lot and headed west, humming.

She had been easy. He had worried about getting to her at her house, but she was such a pitiful little tart that she was the easiest pickup so far. The Hunt had been one of his best. He felt the sure hand of destiny working for him. Maybe he should have branched out to redheads long ago.

The Courtship had been marginal. He would have been more comfortable with the music playing, but maybe she was right. It might have attracted the attention of the old man.

He giggled again. Driving with his usual care, he thought about just how well his plans were working. He relished the memory of Nosy Parker's anguished face when she told him they had arrested Steve. The old bitch had been frantic. He had acted concerned and listened to her, bawling like a cow with a lost calf. "Cow" was just the right word. Nick had almost felt sorry for Steve.

He heard a change in the redhead's breathing. She stirred

and her eyes opened. Good. He didn't want her too badly damaged for the rest of the ritual. He glanced at the passenger seat. It was fitting that her own leather straps bound her hands and feet. He was sure that was one more sign that he was doing the right thing. Yes indeed.

The seat belt held her upright. He had fixed that, too, so it wouldn't budge if she leaned forward. He knew from experience that it would hold her no matter how much she struggled.

She shook her head slowly as if to clear it, then slumped back, sliding her eyes toward him. Mercifully, she stayed silent. He kept humming as he drove, now and then murmuring the words:

"The Farmer takes a wife, the Farmer takes a wife . . . "

Chapter

23

Sweat trickled down Marissa's back, and she had to struggle to keep control of her bowels. She shook from her core outward, like some spasming animal caught in a deadly trap.

Her first impulse had been to fight blindly, but as she struggled back to consciousness, she started to form a plan. Rule Three applied. Since she was in no position to run, she would have to outsmart him. If she could keep him talking, maybe she could find a chance to get away. At least she would save her strength for when it might do her some good.

"Where are you taking me?" Marissa's throat ached, but she managed to keep her tone almost pleasant.

Nick seemed to be considering how he should answer. He shut his eyes for just a second and took a deep breath, then pursed his lips and released the pent-up air. It made a sound that suggested both resignation and regret.

"Marissa, you scared me. You started all that wild talk about missing girls. I was afraid you would do something to get me in trouble, and I haven't done anything wrong. You must know that. They arrested some kid named Steve for hurting those girls." He paused for a second. "I'm awfully sorry that I had to hurt you."

"It's okay," Marissa said in a raspy croak. She wondered how much permanent damage he might have done with his elbow. "I only thought you might be able to help. Gloria is my friend. I'm worried about her."

He smiled gently at the darkness beyond the reach of his headlights. "You don't need to worry about Gloria," he said.

The hot sweat turned clammy. Marissa shivered.

"Why don't you pull over and help me out of these straps," she suggested. "You can trust me. I can't run anyway, and I don't have any idea where we are."

"Let's be real clear about this, Marissa. I'm not stupid. The straps stay on."

"At least talk to me. Tell me where we're going."

"Oh, sure." Nick's voice took on a casual tone, as if they were chatting about plans for a picnic. "I'm taking you to River's Bend." When Marissa didn't respond, he explained. "It's my secret hideaway. My mother died last summer, and I inherited her cabin in the woods. She used to take me there when I was a little boy. We'll spend the night, and when the sun comes up tomorrow morning, you'll go home."

"Did you take the others there?"

"Yes, and each one got home safely. You'll be in good company."

She stretched her legs out. There was room. She might be able to kick out the window if she hit it hard enough with her good leg. Probably she would just make him furious. She was obviously not as strong as he was. She vowed to be smarter.

"Are you going to rape me?" Somehow she made it sound neutral.

Nick actually looked hurt!

"Of course not. That would ruin everything. You have to be pure for the Dispensation."

"Were the others pure?"

It was as if a different person entered Nick's body. The new Nick moaned and gripped the wheel with trembling hands. His face contorted into a tight grimace, and he squinted, focusing far ahead as if he saw something there in the heart of darkness. His upper body rocked back and forth and he hunched his shoulders. His head nodded as he rocked in rhythm with his moaning. He was alone somewhere, out of her reach.

Marissa knew that she had to shake him free, to get him to talk to her, but the intensity of his private frenzy terrified her. Her own mind refused to track. It flitted from subject to subject like a caged bird. She forced herself to *think*. When she spoke, her voice sounded strained, close to breaking.

"What's a dispensation?"

He pulled in a deep, rattling breath, and his body stilled. "That's when I send you home," he said to the darkness.

He relaxed his shoulders and loosened his grip on the wheel. Gradually the first Nick slipped back, with his boyish charm in place like a new shirt. He leaned back against the seat and steered with his left hand, resting his right hand lightly on Marissa's knee.

"I want you to see the cabin. I've been fixing it up for someone special, someone like you. You can tell me what kind of furniture you would like. I want you to be comfortable there."

"My uncle and I are going to a friend's house for Thanksgiving dinner. Will I be home in time?"

He looked surprised and delighted. "Thanksgiving! That's perfect. Oh, Marissa, I have so much to be thankful for. Now don't you worry a bit. I'll send you home at sunrise."

"I don't think I believe you, Nick," she said quietly.

Her breathing had steadied and she felt an odd calm. He had switched from Mysterious Stranger to monster almost instantly. If she could trigger the change, she might have some control over him. Maybe she could use his rage as a weapon. She pushed just a bit harder. "I think you hurt my friend, and those other girls, too. No matter what you do to me, they'll catch you and they'll punish you."

Nick's face changed first. Marissa watched in cold horror as he writhed in his seat and began his strange moaning again. The rasping sound rattled his whole frame. Then he multiplied her horror by smiling tenderly.

His eyes crinkled in a caricature of adoring fondness as he said, "Don't be afraid, darling. Nothing can hurt us as long as we have each other." He winked in slow motion, elaborately, in a parody of shared secrets and confidences. "All I need is you."

A chill marched up from the base of Marissa's spine and settled around her ears. The hair on her arms stood erect.

They rushed forward into darkness. The tires spun across

120

the pavement, making a sound like a strong wind through pine trees. His headlights cut wedges out of the night.

He drove, moaning softly. He seemed to have retreated into some remote internal world. He was hardly aware of her. Marissa searched her mind but could find no way to reach him, either physically or through words. For now, he was too far away in every sense. She watched him warily, wondering how she would find the strength to fight him when the opportunity came. She tested the straps around her wrists and ankles. They held. She leaned her head back against the seat and sighed silently. Her left leg ached.

The car slowed, then turned. The sound of tires on pavement gave way to the rattle of gravel, then a hollow thumping. Marissa looked out at heavy wood beams. They must be crossing a bridge. She glanced down and saw a moonlit flash of water.

Thank goodness for the full moon. Her determination resolved itself into a solid core, graced by hope. She would need light when she got away.

The road on the other side of the bridge turned east, following the river. At first the car traveled smoothly over hard-packed earth. After a few miles it began to buck like a boat in a gale, knocked this way and that by deep ruts.

Nick still clutched the wheel and looked straight ahead. His bestial moans droned on, changing now and then in pitch or tempo. It slowly dawned on her that he wasn't moaning at all. There was a regular rhythm to the sounds. He was humming!

"What's the tune?" she asked.

Nick blinked and looked at her, then answered solemnly,

"It's an old nursery tune my mother used to sing. The words change, depending on what's happening in the game."

He didn't explain further, but he stopped humming and relaxed behind the wheel. He drove in silence for a while, then slowed the car and peered off to the right. A sudden twist of the wheel took them off the road. They came out of deep woods into a grassy area that appeared to be open on three sides. Nick parked the car in front of a tumbledown shack. Marissa could hear the distant sound of moving water when he stopped the engine.

"Welcome to River's Bend," he said. His voice betrayed a landowner's pride. "This is a choice lot. The river flows on three sides of us. The only way out is by the road we came in on."

He stretched lazily, then casually reached into the backseat, bringing out a plastic box. Uncle Paul had a similar one that he used to carry his fishing gear. Nick switched on an electric lantern. Marissa blinked back tears and watched him slowly open the tackle box.

As the lid lifted, a tray about two-inches deep accordioned out toward her. In the tray was a row of squat little jars full of clear liquid. He picked one out and held it close to her face. She could see small blunt objects floating in the liquid. They were pasty white and wrinkled. They were tipped with glossy red, almost like . . .

Marissa gagged. It was like a hidden-picture puzzle. Suddenly she recognized what she was seeing and couldn't imagine how she hadn't known immediately. Each jar held five severed toes.

Chapter

24

Marissa fought back the scream that threatened to consume her. She didn't dare to lose control. Hunching forward, she bowed her head and squeezed her eyes shut. She struggled to keep from vomiting. Fighting her blossoming horror, she was barely aware of Nick sliding out of the car and coming around to her side. The door opened and a rush of cold air slapped her sweat-drenched skin. She tensed. This could be her chance.

Nick was still mostly in his charming phase, but he was like a cracked cup. The monster inside seeped through. The combined charmer-beast was more bizarre than either could have been by itself. He acted with caricatured courtesy, as if he had lost control of the boundaries of this personality.

"Let me help you, my love," Nick whispered. He bent as if he would actually have kissed her hand. They might have been on their way to a formal dance or dinner party. His dimple flashed as he reached across her and released the seat belt.

Marissa brought her bound arms up ferociously and twisted

left. Her elbow struck his chin. His head jerked back, and the monster took full possession. He roared and grabbed at her, but she fell away from him across the driver's seat. She pulled her knees close to her chest and kicked with all her strength. She caught him in the stomach and drove him back. He fell, cursing.

She hadn't heard his door close. Please, please be open, she thought, and she pushed again with her bound legs, finding purchase against the door frame. Her shoulders hit the driver's-side door and it swung open.

Marissa rolled out, hitting the ground with a painful thump. She wriggled across the wet ground toward the under-growth and beneath the prickly leaves of Oregon Grape. Huddled there, she groped frantically to unbuckle the strap around her ankles. It snapped open. She struggled to her feet clumsily, hindered as much by having her arms tied together as by her awkward leg.

She stumbled deeper into the woods. On her third step, her balance failed. Her weight shifted slightly downhill and she tumbled heavily to the ground again. She grunted when the air rushed out of her lungs, but she didn't cry out.

Nick must have heard her thrashing in the darkness. He was on her like a raving animal, shouting his rage and pummeling her with his fists. The monster was in full control.

Marissa cowered, trying to protect her head with her arms. His first rage subsided and he stood over her, panting. He held the leather strap in his left hand. It made a smacking sound as he struck it against his right palm, then he raised it high.

The blows rained down, punctuated by wordless roars that

124

seemed to rise from his throat like a throng of desperate beasts escaping into the night. Gradually she made sense out of the terrible sounds.

"You've been bad! Bad! Bad! Bad!"

With each repetition the strap fell upon her raised arms, her head, her shoulders. Her sweater and jacket absorbed some of the punishing force, but the sheer terror she felt made her more vulnerable. An image of the old woman flashed through her mind, spitting on the ground and calling her cursed. She was embraced by despair.

Her head hurt. She was cold. Her shoulders spoke in razor tongues. Light came strongly from her right; then shadows fluttered across her line of vision. He stood before her. The Mysterious Stranger was back.

"I'm so sorry, Marissa, but you know that you were very bad and you hurt me. You forced me to hit you because I care about you so much. Can you understand that?"

She looked up at him and managed to nod. Her arms were shackled to metal brackets on the wall above her head. Her feet barely reached the floor; she had to rest her weight on her toes, with her heels raised in the air. The lift on her sneaker didn't help her short leg at all in this position. Her left leg screamed protests that were echoed faintly by her arms.

She rolled her head to the left and inspected her prison. She was in a crude rectangular shelter with two glassless windows and a door on the opposite wall. The other walls had no windows, but whole planks were absent, and the wind blew through them freely. The roof was partly missing, but it provided some protection from the constant drip of the coastal forest.

Two wood crates supported a makeshift shelf about five feet away, and a third stood on the floor directly in front of her. A wood chair with layers of paint showing through chips and gouges stood beside the shelf.

Drifts of pine needles carpeted the corners. The place smelled of mouse droppings and old urine.

The shelf held an electric lantern that cast light and shadows around the shelter. A large gym bag lay beside the tackle box, which was, mercifully, closed. Marissa shuddered and tried to convince herself that Nick's collection was fake. It had to be fake. No one in his right mind would carry around someone's toes.

Involuntarily her own toes moved down to press against the floor. He must have seen the motion. He approached her with an expression of tender concern.

"Are you comfortable? Oh, how you scared me, Marissa. Running off into the dark woods like that! I was sure you'd get lost or hurt yourself. There are wild animals out there. You really frightened me. Thank goodness I found you. Now you're safe in the cabin. I know you'll like it here."

She could hardly bear to look at his face. It was incredible to her that he still looked like the handsome young man she had first seen on the carousel. He talked as if they were friends sharing a minor adventure.

They were in two contradictory universes. Oddly, Marissa thought, hers had been turned inside out like a terrible dream., while his was the normal world where good manners count for something.

Nick went on in the same solicitous tone. "I'm sorry I can't offer you something to eat. I haven't had a chance to fix up the kitchen. I was hoping you might have some ideas."

He smiled at her as if he had a wonderful secret to share, and opened the gym bag. "I brought everything else we need, though."

He took out a lace cloth and shook it open with a snap, then tenderly spread it across the crate in front of her. He fussed with the edges to be sure they draped just right. Marissa watched his shadow dancing crazily across the walls.

The next thing out of the bag was a pair of latex gloves, which he placed in the center of the cloth. He looked a bit apologetic when he saw her staring at the gloves. "Please don't think I don't respect you. It's always better to be safe. Do you agree?"

It took a second for the shock of realization to hit her. Marissa had listened politely to Ms. Martinez's lectures on safe sex, but she had always figured that she wouldn't have much to worry about on that score. Nick was thinking of the gloves as condoms!

She gagged when he took the next item out of the bag. It was an ice pick.

He carefully laid it across the gloves, then reached into the bag again and withdrew something Marissa recognized from Uncle Paul's shop: bolt cutters.

"I had to borrow these from your workshop," Nick said. "I

left my last pair in a friend's car." He giggled softly, then watched her face intently while he drew the large handles apart. He grinned and slammed them together. "Snick, snick," he said.

He laid them on the crate and reached into the bag again, removing something that looked like a carving. Marissa saw that it was a little model of a carousel horse standing on its rear legs—a prancer. It was on top of a round platform with a key protruding from the side.

The winding mechanism made a clicking sound when Nick turned the key. He set the little horse on the lace cloth and stood back to watch it rotate. Tinkling music began, delicate and airy as mist. It was "The Carousel Waltz."

The tiny sound was almost lost in the winter woods. To Marissa, the little horse sounded achingly lonely.

Nick's eyes grew dreamy. "That music always reminds me of happy times," he said. "My mother used to take me to the carousel in Emerson Park, but only if I was very good. Sometimes she made me ride all afternoon."

Marissa watched a single tear meander across his cheek. "Some little children don't like carousels," she said. "They can get awfully scared."

"That's what the strap is for," he answered. A second tear followed the first.

The elegant little tune slowed and stopped. Nick wiped his face. "We have lots of time, Marissa. It won't be dawn for another four hours. Let's get better acquainted." His gaze was direct and his smile sincere. "Maybe you would enjoy some company. We'll need witnesses for the ceremony."

He opened the tackle box and took out his collection of little jars, arranging them in a semicircle behind the carousel figure. A half dozen flashy bracelets tinkled against each other as he slipped them over one of the jars. The last thing he picked up was a ring. It caught the light as he placed it on top of the center jar.

Marissa recognized Gloria's opal.

Chapter 25

Cindy woke slowly with an uneasy feeling. Odd light filtered through the window. Was it morning? The color was wrong for daylight. She reluctantly sat up, wincing when her feet touched the cold floor. Her uneasiness grew. She didn't stop for slippers but walked barefooted to the window, as Marissa had done three hours earlier. It was still dark outside, but the carousel lights glowed.

"Marissa!" she called out. "What's going on?"

Half an hour later, flashing lights played across Salmon Creek Park. Cindy thought the world had gone topsy-turvy. The light ought to be coming from the carousel, but instead it came from a patrol car. Instead of band-organ music, she listened to staccato voices blaring from the police radio. Marissa was supposed to be safe in bed, but the bed had been empty and cold.

Cindy opened the door to the state troopers gratefully. "It doesn't make any sense," she said to the two officers. They stood together under the parking-lot light. "If Marissa went anywhere on her own, she would have taken Prancer."

Seeing their puzzled expressions, she pointed to the little Volkswagen, which looked utterly alone to Cindy. "Her car. That's its name. She would have taken it if she had left on her own. Something's terribly wrong."

Within five minutes, one of the officers was speaking into his car radio. "We have another missing girl, only this one's a redhead." He repeated Cindy's description of Marissa.

When he came back, he said, "It's a good thing you called us right away. We'll have your friend's description on all the state news services within the hour and all the law enforcement people will be on the lookout. If she's anywhere in the state, I think we'll find her."

Chapter

26

"I'm cold," Marissa said. She was shivering in spite of her sweater and jacket. She was sure the shivering wasn't entirely related to the temperature.

Nick's voice droned on, as if she hadn't spoken. "We spent lots of weekends up here when I was growing up. When I was good, Mother let me go fishing and took me on hikes. When I was bad, of course, I had to be punished. She made me stay in the cabin all day. Sometimes she used the chain to be sure I didn't wander off into the woods. That would have been dangerous, and very bad.

"Sometimes she had to use the straps, but she only punished me because she loved me so much. It was best for me in the long run. She was right about that. She was a good mother. She never hurt me unless I really needed it."

He was seated on the battered chair across the little table from Marissa. The ankle of his right leg was propped on his left knee. He bent toward her, his head cocked to the left. His eyes were alive with reflected light. He reminded Marissa of a ferret she had seen in the biology lab at school.

His fingers drummed on his calf, and his foot rose and fell in cadence with his words. The cadence seemed to shift, depending on what he was talking about. He spoke of the woods with a *tap-pause-tap* rhythm. When he spoke of his mother, the beat was *tap-tap-tap*.

"Did I tell you she died last summer? Yes indeed. She died and left me River's Bend. Now I can come here anytime I want to. I'll fix it up next summer and make it real livable."

"Does it have an outhouse?" Marissa asked softly. "I really need to go to the bathroom."

Nick's dimple grew deeper and he smiled at her benignly. His eyes took on a faraway expression. He continued as if she hadn't spoken.

"Yes, next year I'll have to fix up a bathroom. I'm considering ruffled curtains. Mother loved ruffles."

His foot tapped faster.

"I was hoping you could help me with ideas for furniture." Nick nodded toward the jars. "They weren't any help at all."

He smiled with a brilliance that would have stopped her heart with joy just the day before. Now she thought it was more likely to stop her heart with terror. She was still half hanging from her arms. The calf muscle of her left leg jerked, but when she slumped to rest her leg, metal dug into her wrists.

Nick noticed her discomfort and smiled regretfully. "I was about your size the last time I had to be punished with the shackles. It was dawn before my mother got back that time."

He bowed his head, and Marissa looked down on the curls that lay softly against his neck. She shivered again, this time with revulsion.

"Are you warm enough? Shall I turn up the fire?"

Marissa was miserably cold, and she ached everywhere. She had had enough of his phony consideration. Before she thought, the part of her that believed in being a realist spoke.

"There is no fire and this isn't a cabin. It's a run-down shack that wouldn't keep a rat warm."

As soon as the words were out, she regretted them.

This time there was no leaking of personalities. Nick's transformation was instantaneous. His teeth bared, and his eyes narrowed. He jumped up, knocking over the chair, and screamed.

"Shut up, shut up!" The volume rose steadily. "You ungrateful little turd! You don't know when you're lucky, that's what's wrong with you. You're lucky and you don't even know it. You have doo-doo for brains, that's what you have. Doo-doo for brains!"

In spite of her terror, Marissa had a weird urge to laugh. Doo-doo! He really was crazy.

He shrieked and slammed the chair against the empty door frame; it shattered. Holding the splintered leg in one hand, he whirled toward her and spat on her face. He grabbed the top of her ear and twisted hard. Marissa couldn't help crying out in pain. He waved the chair leg like a club, back and forth, inches from her face. She flattened herself against the wall.

Nick screamed into her face, "Look what you made me do. You'll have to be punished for that."

He slammed the chair leg against the wall beside her head, so hard her ears rang. Six feet tall to her five, he towered over her. She cringed. He stood over her and glowered.

A deep, shuddering breath, then another, brought him back into control. He stepped away from her and sighed. Charming Nick was back. He laughed easily and slipped his hands into his pockets. "We can do that later."

Goodwill drew across his face like a curtain. His scimitar gaze turned to silk as his eyes caressed her. Little smile lines appeared, and his lips parted slightly to show flawless teeth. He expanded the smile into a boyish grin and softened his voice.

"We have to get ready. Soon it will be time for your Dispensation."

He kicked the splintered chair aside and took a hairbrush out of his gym bag. Turning toward her, he whispered her name. "Marissa. It's a beautiful name, and you're a beautiful girl. We just need to fix you up a little for the ceremony."

He came to stand close beside her and ran the brush through her hair. He pulled on the bow, releasing the pale green ribbon, and ran its length through his fingers. "This suits you," he said. "Beautiful and innocent." He rested his right hand on the wall beside her head.

Marissa forced herself to be still. She yearned to sink her teeth into his exposed wrist, but she concentrated on being patient. She didn't have much in the way of weapons: her teeth, Cindy's knife, her own wits. Her most powerful weapon

135

was provided by Nick himself. If she could choose her time exactly right, she could use his awful rage against him. Timing her move would be tricky. His transformations were getting more rapid and less predictable.

He was watching her. With enormous effort, she lifted her chin high. It wasn't too late for Rule One.

"I'm sorry I hit you earlier, sweetheart," Nick whispered.

He was so close that she could feel his heat. Her nostrils filled with his oily animal scent.

"You upset me. I lost control for a second." He reached up and stroked her cheek tenderly. "Please forgive me. I only did it because I love you so much." He brushed her hair back from her face, then carefully retied the ribbon.

"This color enhances the glory of your hair," he murmured. "I think you may turn out to be the perfect one."

"Perfect" was a word that Marissa had never considered for herself. He must be blind as well as crazy.

"I'm hardly perfect," she said.

Nick looked bewildered. "Do you mean you aren't pure?"

Marissa laughed. Fat chance of that. "No, that isn't what I mean. I mean my body isn't perfect. It's deformed. My leg . . . "

He dropped his chin and frowned down at her jeans-clad legs. Slowly comprehension dawned. "You limp a little, don't you? Have you been hurt?"

His voice was full of honest sympathy. Marissa was astonished. He had entirely missed the most important thing about her. Obviously it wasn't so important, at least not to him. She almost allowed a bitter laugh. What a time to find that out!

Marissa decided to push her luck while he seemed to be listening. "No. I was born this way." She paused, then plunged ahead. "Please," she said. "I need to go to the bathroom."

She hardly dared to believe it when Nick casually reached up and unbuckled the straps that fastened her wrists. Cautioning herself to be patient, she stood very still.

He gently stroked her forehead, brushing her curls back with tender care, as if she were a doll. He leaned back a little and regarded her.

If she could provoke him into a tantrum and use her small size to evade him, she might have a single chance in a thousand of breaking free. She was absolutely certain of one thing: If she didn't try it, escape had a probability of zero.

She forced herself to smile. "Thanks, Nick. I really do need to go to the bathroom."

She forced a little-girl look onto her face and even managed to blink slowly, trying for childlike appeal and thinking that she could playact charm almost as well as he could. She reached for his hand, ignoring its slimy coldness, and pleaded with her eyes. "Help me?"

Marissa rubbed her wrists to restore circulation and leaned back against the wall. Nick put a hand on her elbow to offer support. She took a step and staggered a bit, falling against him. He put his arm around her shoulders.

"Thank you," she said. Her legs were stiff and they tingled with returning blood flow. Her shoulders ached. She glanced at her watch. It was nearly five o'clock in the morning. She had been safe in bed just four hours ago. She thought ruefully about Cindy, still blissfully asleep. They would never know what had happened to her.

Marissa didn't dare think about that, or about Cindy and Uncle Paul. She would paralyze herself with fear if she considered how much she had to lose. She concentrated on Nick, trying to read his expression, focusing solely on him. She presented him with what she hoped was a flirtatious glance. "You're very strong."

Nick beamed. Stopping to pick up the lantern, he led her to the door. The sill was about two feet above the forest floor. If there had ever been steps, time and weather had rotted them away. He hesitated and looked out warily before he stepped out.

In the part of a second when he looked away, Marissa slipped her right hand into her jeans pocket. The little knife was still there, warm from long contact with her leg. It was like a thin rope in a turbulent sea, physically fragile but enough, perhaps, to save her. She slid it out and flicked the little blade up with her thumbnail.

Nick put the lantern on the ground and turned to her with his arms wide. Reaching up, he grasped her waist and effortlessly swung her down, setting her on her feet like Fred Astaire assisting Ginger Rogers.

She wrapped her left arm around his neck, looked up at him adoringly, and whispered, "Thanks," as she drove the knife into the side of his neck.

He bellowed and dropped her. With the knife still in her hand, she tumbled into a crouch, then struggled to get both feet beneath her, and ran. He chased her with rage pouring out of him like an erupting volcano. She ducked around the edge of the shack. There was his car!

She tried the driver's-side door. Locked! Supporting her weak leg with her hand, she bolted crookedly away from the clearing and into the forest. The welcoming dark received her.

Nick stood beside his car and shouted, calling Marissa every foul name she had ever heard and some she had only heard in movies. She was relieved to hear the outpouring of filth. "Doo-doo" had spooked her.

She crouched in a hollow at the base of a big Douglas fir, wriggling to bury herself in the thick pine-needle duff. She fought to breathe quietly as silence descended on the forest. A dreadful moaning started, faint, then growing stronger. Nick was humming again.

He came to the edge of the clearing, holding the light high and peering into the shadow-quickened forest.

"Marissa," he called. "I'm afraid you've been very, very bad. I don't want to have to punish you, Marissa, but I will if you force me to. Be good and come out now."

She cringed back into deeper shadow and watched him pacing and peering at the edge of the open space around the cabin. When he let the lantern hang down, the upward-streaming light turned his handsome face into a grotesque, with diabolical eyebrows that cast shadows up across his forehead. Like a fawn at the approach of a wolf, Marissa didn't move.

Nick went to his car and unlocked the door. Marissa dared

to hope that he might drive away, but he simply leaned in and turned on the headlights.

She put up her arms to shield her eyes from the sudden onslaught of light. The motion must have caught his attention. He waved gaily and called out, "There you are, love. I was afraid I wouldn't find you."

He lunged toward her, crashing right through the low-growing Oregon Grape. Something caught his foot. He fell full-length, and the lantern skittered toward her.

Marissa grabbed it and heaved it high and backward over her head. She heard it crash to the earth as she dodged a tree and ran, away from the headlights and parallel to the road through the forest.

The ground was covered with shrubs and fallen branches. It wasn't raining, but everything was wet. In places the forest floor sloped steeply, and the pine needles were as slippery as oil. Marissa almost laughed when she realized that having a short leg was hardly a disadvantage here. The ground was so uneven that anyone would have uncertain footing. She used her arms to pull herself through a dense thicket of small firs. Branches slapped her, and once she twisted her good ankle on a loose rock. She tumbled to the ground and landed hard.

She sat for a moment, struggling to catch her breath. Branches snapped behind her, and she heard Nick's heavy footfalls. Out of the direct rays of his headlights, the forest lay in patches of deep shadow and dim light. The electric lantern had gone out when it landed. Now he was as hampered by darkness as she was. The odds were a bit more even.

Light waxed and waned as scudding clouds revealed, then

obscured, the full moon. Marissa pulled the little notebook and pen out of her pocket and wrote in the wavering light.

Help me, please! The one who's killing all those girls had me but I got away. His name is Nick Farmer.

Marissa squeezed her eyes shut and tried hard to remember Nick's license-plate number. She was uncertain of the last two digits, but she wrote down her best guess and added a question mark.

At least she was certain of her own name. She signed the note *Marissa Beth Bruner.* Her mother's name had been Beth.

She crept away from the river's murmuring flow. Belly down on the damp forest floor, she crawled to the verge of the logging road.

She watched for a while, alert for any sign of Nick. Nothing moved. She grabbed a madrone branch and pulled herself up, then tugged the ribbon out of her hair and stretched to tie it to a higher branch. She tugged her mother's ring off her finger. She kissed it with her eyes closed; then, with trembling fingers, she tied it to the middle of the ribbon. It dangled over the road, spinning slowly. Finally Marissa tied her note to the ribbon's end with a quick knot and retreated from the exposed roadbed.

It was a slim chance, but elk hunters and people looking for Christmas trees might be on the road, even on Thanksgiving Day. The diamond might catch someone's eye, even if the note did not. Her hand felt naked without the ring, but Marissa had no time to mourn its loss. She leaned against a tree and tried to think.

Like opening curtains, the clouds moved aside. Moonlight

filled the forest. Marissa could see the vague outlines of pine branches. Something drifted down in front of her, floating from left to right. It was soft and white, and she suddenly became aware that she was very cold.

It was snowing.

He stood in the shelter of a cedar tree and watched fat snowflakes tumble toward the ground. They lingered for a moment, then vanished. He remembered another snowfall, long ago.

His mother's voice. He was certain he heard his mother's voice, calling through the storm. "Boy! Boy-o! You come back now, hear?"

He dropped into a low crouch, resting his forehead on his knees, and whimpered. His fingers clenched, relaxed, then clenched again. He felt the bite of snowflakes on his bare neck.

"Little Nick, you know you have been bad. So bad. You know Mama has to punish you, so you might as well come now. If I have to come out there after you, things will only be worse. If you come in now, Mama may not have to pinch you so hard."

He wailed. He cowered and waited for his mother's firm hand to fall on his neck. He knew she would pinch him, and he knew where she would pinch hardest. He huddled lower, protecting himself. The snow fell.

Cold stabbed him. He was wet. He was afraid he had soiled himself in his fear. Oh, this was going to be terrible. He would be in such bad trouble!

As if he were watching a movie screen, that awful night played itself out in his mind. He had hidden in the snowy woods since just after dark. At dawn he heard her humming a familiar nursery tune. The sound came closer, and he couldn't run away. His legs were so cold, so stiff. He felt paralyzed. He flattened himself in a hollow among the roots of a tree and prayed to become invisible.

Just as the first rays of the sun burst through the pines, his mother found him. He remembered it very well.

Slowly he became aware of a moaning sound. It was his own voice, humming. He rose shakily and brushed the dirt from his pants legs. He had to find the redhead in time for the Dispensation.

144

Chapter 28

She heard him laughing.

"This is perfect, Marissa," Nick called out. Then he started to sing.

> "The farmer's girl has gone
> She left him all alone.
> But when the farmer finds her
> He will send his girl-o home."

He giggled. "Are you ready to come back and take your punishment, Marissa? You won't feel right unless you do."

Snowflakes clung to fir boughs and, like the carousel's mirrors, multiplied the glow of the full moon. The night was pale with reflected light. Marissa could see her way more easily, but she knew Nick would be able to see her, too.

She stayed off the road but hoped to get far enough ahead of him that she could chance using it instead of the difficult path through the underbrush. Her face was wet with snowflakes and tears, and even though she was wearing her sneaker with the lift, her left leg was tiring. It ached with cold and fatigue, and her body rocked wildly with every hurried step.

A boulder jutted out from the forest floor just ahead. She sank to her knees beside it, huddling low to the ground so she would be in deeper shadow. The hard surface of the rock chilled and reassured her at once.

"Cold comfort," she whispered to the rock.

She heard Nick tramping through the forest. He stopped his odd moaning hum now and then to burst into laughter. Then he called to her. "Marissa! Girl-o! You come back now, hear?"

"Please, please," she whispered with her eyes closed against the sparkling night. "Please go away."

She hoped he wouldn't find her ring on the madrone tree. She hoped that a helicopter would appear out of the sky and shine a spotlight on him. While she was at it, she hoped some superhero would fly down to carry her off to safety.

This was crazy. Marissa squeezed her eyes even more tightly shut and tried to think. She couldn't outrun him. How could she ever outsmart him?

Nick's humming stopped. She opened her eyes. He stood just five feet away. He had a coil of rope hanging from his right shoulder. His legs were planted wide apart. A trickle of blood made a dark smear on his neck. He smiled at her.

"Hello, girl-o. It's time to send you home."

Marissa struggled to her feet and ran. He was right behind her. She dodged a tree and slipped down a slope toward the road. Her left leg faltered. She clutched it with her left hand, supporting it, and at the same time demanding more from herself than she ever had before. Then she made a mistake; she broke Rule Two. She turned around to see where he was and didn't notice a low branch. Hard wood smacked the side of her head and sent her sprawling.

Nick dropped on her like a hawk on a mouse. With one knee on each side of her hips, he wrapped the rope around and around her upper body, pinning her arms. He yanked on the rope, forcing Marissa to her feet. She fell, and he pulled her up again. Through all of this, he never said a word, and he never stopped smiling.

He guided her out of the woods and onto the rutted road. She was suddenly aware of predawn light scattered across the sky. It was a little easier to find her footing on the rough road. A brief flash of colored light startled her. It was her ring, hanging in full view less than twenty feet ahead. She had to distract him.

"What's the hurry, Nick?"

"Sunrise," he snarled. "It's nearly time for sunrise. The Dispensation is always at sunrise."

"I can't see my watch," she lied. "What time is it?"

"Nearly seven. Hurry up!" He prodded her, but more gently.

She breathed and hurried past the tree. Gloria's sea-green ribbon fluttered like a banner, but Marissa's distraction had worked. Nick didn't notice it or her mother's flashing diamond. Maybe someday someone would find it, and they would know then what had happened to her.

In another five minutes they reached River's Bend. Marissa

was amazed that she had managed to get so far in the dark. If she had been able to run like a normal person, it might even have been far enough.

He urged her toward a Douglas fir and wrapped a loop of the rope around it. Leaving her tied there, he disappeared into his cabin.

The clearing in front of the cabin was about fifty feet across and flat. Trees filled the area behind her, between the clearing and the road. On the other three sides, the land appeared to drop off. Marissa thought she could hear the susurration of water as it moved over the riverbed. At one time the cabin must have been lovingly located in the river's embrace. She wondered what could have gone so terribly wrong.

Light tinged the southeastern sky. Distant mountains were outlined by approaching dawn. She didn't have much time.

A dim plan formed out of the confusion in her mind, a plan with almost zero probability of success. She had no idea how far down the water might be, or how deep, or whether there were rocks at the base of the embankment. She did know two things: She would rather jump off the edge of the earth than stay for Nick's dispensation, and she didn't dare to jump into water wearing a heavy sweater, jacket, and sneakers.

She was already numb with cold, but she would have to find a way to get rid of some of her clothes. The idea of undressing in front of Nick made her shudder with a deeper cold, one rising from within; but unless she could come up with a better plan, that was what she must do.

The new light revealed rectangular dark areas in the grassy clearing. Marissa didn't waste time pretending they were caused by anything in nature. Any realist would recognize the shapes. When she realized that she must be looking at graves, any hesitation she had felt dissolved. She would do whatever she must to survive.

Nick was humming when he returned, carrying his gym bag in one hand and the wood crate in the other. He set the crate down and once more fussed over the lace cloth, ignoring Marissa while he arranged it to his satisfaction.

He leered at her when he pulled out the latex gloves. Then he picked up the ice pick and ran his fingers over the spike thoughtfully. He approached her, holding the sharp tip erect so that it was just inches from her eyes. She blinked reflexively and shrank back against the tree.

"Your eyes are green, like emeralds. Don't they call emeralds 'green ice'?" His gentle smile hardened into a brittle line as he laid the ice pick next to the gloves. Then he looked at her with a puzzled expression. "What happened to your ribbon? It was the same green as your eyes."

"I don't know. I—I must have lost it in the woods," Marissa stammered. He didn't question her further. He probably thought she was simply afraid. Well, she was.

She watched Nick arrange his dreadful little jars and lay the bolt cutters next to them. He opened his car trunk and lifted out a heavy sledgehammer. Measuring her with his eyes, he placed two huge spikes on the ground, about three feet apart. He studied her for a moment, then moved one of the stakes about three inches closer to the other. Once more he approached her, standing close so that he dwarfed her.

"You're just a little squirt, aren't you?" He sounded

friendly, as if Marissa were a girl he was flirting with at a dance. She stared at the ground, afraid that if she looked into his eyes she would betray her fear and rage. That was not part of the plan. It was best to humor him, for now.

He carefully positioned the other two stakes and pulled four leather straps out of his gym bag. He knelt to attach one to each of the stakes. Marissa could imagine someone her size lying at the center of the rectangle, with arms and legs spread-eagled. In her imagination she could see Gloria there, helpless and terrified. Anything would be better than that.

Finally Nick went into the cabin and came out with the carousel music box cradled in his hand. He wound it with a rasping sound and set it on top of the crate.

The music box began its fragile tune. Nick stopped his monotonous humming and stood before the bizarre altar. His chin rested on his chest. His eyelids were squeezed into trembling slits. His hands hung, tightly clenched, at his sides. Drawing in a shuddering breath, he turned toward Marissa. His eyes glistened with tears, and also with an awful eagerness. It was the eagerness she had seen in his face when he brought girls to the carousel, only magnified a hundred times. He moved toward her as if in a trance and stood so close she could smell the sour sweat on him.

He studied her face, then sighed deeply and murmured, "You may be the perfect one."

She couldn't answer, and in the silence she became aware of a distant roar. It was different from the river's sound, more robust than soughing wind through trees. Marissa's heart thumped and her neck stiffened. It was, unmistakably, a car. She screamed.

Nick slapped her with his open hand. Her head jerked back and hit the tree. Stars danced in her vision. The sound of the passing car dwindled, then was gone.

He stood beside her for another moment, threatening with his size and closeness. The river seemed to echo the sound of his labored breath and her quiet sobs. Roughly, and without a word, he untied the rope that bound her to the tree and unwound it from around her straitjacketed arms. He shoved her abruptly. Marissa staggered on her weak leg and collapsed at the center of the sacrificial ground, surrounded by his straps and stakes. She struggled to her knees and forced herself to look up at his face. It was alive with anticipation and triumph. He lifted his chin and gazed toward the southeast. With each passing second the brightness intensified. Only a few clouds were left, drifting high overhead. The snow had stopped and there was no threat of rain. It would be a lovely sunrise.

"Let me undress for you," Marissa whispered. When he looked at her in disbelief, she said it again. "Let me undress."

She watched Nick's astonishment give way to uncertain delight. "Maybe you really do understand. It's possible. You might be the one I've searched for all along."

Marissa planted her backside on the wet grass and pulled off her sneakers and socks, then braced herself with her hands on the cold earth and rose unsteadily to her feet. Keeping her eyes locked to his, she edged away from the area outlined by the four stakes, toward the river. She forced herself to move slowly, thinking of him as a wild creature that she must not startle.

She put on a mask of charm. She licked her lips and willed them to relax into a smile. She put a facade of adoring fascination into her eyes. She kept her face immobile, as if she were aware only of Nick. Her mind worked frantically to keep her body moving, every so slowly, toward the riverbank. She didn't look in the direction of the graves.

"Let me do it my way." She tried to sound seductive. "If this is what I have to do, I want to do it right."

He watched her as if he were hypnotized. "You're the first to understand," he whispered. "The moment of calm at the end is part of the gift. The others gave in, finally, but you are the first to be willing. You must be the one."

Marissa could sense the edge of the riverbank behind her. Its sound was louder; the earth felt softer. The sunlight coming over her shoulder illuminated Nick's face, turning his eyes a vivid blue. He took one step toward her, then another.

"Wait there," she whispered. "I want to dance for you."

He stopped. His breathing was more regular now. His eyes were like rivets, holding her to him.

Marissa fought to recall everything she had ever seen or heard about dancing, swallowing the bitter irony that she who could never dance was forced to do it to save herself. She drew in a deep breath of cold air. Swinging her hips as much as she could without losing her balance, she put her weight on her left leg and willed it to hold her. She lifted her right foot and tapped the earth. Then, emphasizing the hip movement, she balanced on her right leg and touched her left foot to the ground. Right, then left again, her feet tapped and her hips swayed in a hulalike motion. Her undulating hips kept Nick's eyes fastened on her. His mouth dropped open slightly.

Slowly, ever so slowly, she shrugged out of her jacket. She dropped it gently on the ground, her eyes never leaving his. Then she dropped her hands to the hem of her sweater. For a moment she hesitated. She took a chance on breaking eye contact and glanced behind her. The river rushed by, not fifteen feet down. It looked deep. It looked swift. She quickly refocused her gaze on Nick. She had not altered her sultry dance.

He watched her, mesmerized for the moment, but she knew he might break at any time. It worried her that the dance was so sexual. She thought the sensuous part might trigger another passion of rage. He had said he wouldn't rape her, but she had come to understand that rape and killing were the same for him. She must keep him at bay for just a few moments longer.

She pulled the hem of the sweater slowly upward. She hated the idea of having her eyes covered, but she got through it with a swiftness that carried the sweater up and off and onto the ground in a single fluid motion.

Goose bumps sprang up across her arms and shoulders. Her chest heaved. Her breasts were covered only by her usual cotton bra, and the cold reached deep. She managed an inviting smile.

At that instant the sun burst above the mountains and flooded the river valley. It glinted off wet leaves and the few remaining flakes of snow. Nick's blue eyes shone. He blinked.

Now! Marissa threw herself back and out and was swallowed by the river.

Chapter 29

The cold almost paralyzed her. Her head burst through the water and she heard a faraway whimper, like the sound of a trapped animal struggling for air. Was it Nick? She rolled onto her side in the current to get a glimpse upstream. Nick stood on the bank with his legs apart and clenched fists upraised, exactly as Frankenstein's monster had stood in the burning windmill. Between the two monsters, she would prefer to take her chances with the film version.

Nick's mouth moved, but she couldn't hear what he was shouting. All she heard was a whiny cry that ricocheted through her skull. The horrible noise seemed very far away, but she slowly realized that it was coming from her. She listened, as if at a distance, to the sound of air lurching through her constricted throat into her stricken lungs. She had no way to control it.

Marissa's arms and legs gradually began to obey her mind's commands. Her flailing became a rhythmic series of kicks and strokes. She gave herself a moment's mental congratulation for having had enough sense to get rid of her jacket, sweater, and sneakers. They would have filled with water and would surely have drowned her. Well, she probably wouldn't drown, but the cold would kill her almost as quickly. She swam harder.

The water swept her out of sight of Nick and his so-called cabin and carried her along the outside edge of the next curve, bringing her close to the bank. She used its momentum to propel herself toward an undercut section. Her bare feet touched a boulder on the bottom, then another, then the rocky bed of the river. She crawled out of the water, shivering uncontrollably, and huddled beneath the shelter of the over-hanging bank. She looked up at the ceiling of her refuge, into the roots of the tree above.

She was on a bed of grass and pine needles that had been washed ashore by spring floods and were still above the water-line. She wrapped her arms around her knees, trying to conserve every bit of body heat. Her sanctuary wasn't warm, but it was relatively dry. She looked around at the garbage left behind by boaters and the river. Bottle caps and cigarette butts predominated, even here in the wild area. A sheet of plastic wound around a dangling tree root. Marissa scooted over to it and pulled it loose. It was strong clear plastic, perhaps once used as a tent fly or to cover camping supplies.

She unzipped her wet jeans and pulled them off, then rubbed pine needles over her arms and legs to get off as much water as possible. The friction warmed her somewhat, but the shivering was entirely out of her control. She considered taking off her wet underwear, too, but preferred being a little wet to being entirely naked.

She rescued Cindy's knife from her jeans pocket and cut a slit in the plastic. Slipping the sheet over her head, Marissa gathered it around her waist, then searched the tangled roots. With all the fishermen on the river, there must be a piece of line somewhere.

The sun had traveled well above the horizon and now filled Marissa's cavelike shelter with light that glistened on damp grass and sparkled from the silver surface of a discarded beer can. There! A glimmer revealed a knot of plastic line among the heaped debris. Marissa's hands shook violently, but she managed to untangle enough of the line to tie around the waist of her makeshift poncho.

The plastic cover kept the wind from removing her body heat and would keep moisture from the dripping trees away from her skin. She wasn't warm by any means, but she had slowed the rate of heat loss. Her shivering gradually diminished. She had bought herself a few hours of survival, but she knew she could not last very long in the wet cold of the forest.

Marissa left her jeans behind but clutched the knife as she climbed a gentle slope up from the river. The skies had cleared, but the weather could change quickly and bring more snow. Cautiously she crept through the forest toward where she thought the road would be. Her only real hope was to follow it and walk back to the coast highway.

A break in the trees marked the logging road. Marissa figured she was at least half a mile downstream from Nick, maybe as much as a mile. Still, she would have to be careful.

Chapter

30

He screamed into the wind. He had been so ready for this one. She had made him believe that she wanted the Dispensation as much as he did. It had promised to be perfect. He clutched the ice pick in his hand with a death grip.

He sank to his knees at the center of his sacrificial ground. She had betrayed him! Oh yes indeed, she would have to be punished severely. Over and over, he drove the ice pick into the earth where her eyes should have been.

Finally his rage was spent. His knees were wet from kneeling on the ground. The muscles in his arms and face twitched wildly. He stood and looked down the river, toward where he had last seen the girl. He hoped she had drowned like a rat; he only wished that he had been able to watch.

He had to find her. Even if the crippled little slut was already dead, he couldn't afford to have her body discovered so near River's Bend. There would be questions. They might find out he had been bad, and he would be punished. Tears flowed from his perfectly blue eyes.

He put his gym bag and tackle box in the car trunk, where they would be out of sight, then drove out to the logging road. He started to hum.

Chapter
31

Marissa crouched behind a prickly thicket of Oregon Grape and peered down the road. Everything looked different in the daylight. She thought Nick had come upriver after leaving the coast highway. If that was so, the river had given her a boost back toward the bridge they had crossed. She walked with the rising sun at her back, heading, as nearly as she could determine, toward the road that would take her home.

There was no way to keep her feet dry. They were so cold that she could barely feel the ground beneath them. Her hands were numb, too, and her weak leg ached. She lurched along.

One of the boys in Ms. Martinez's health class had done an oral report on hypothermia. Marissa remembered him saying that people lost in the woods could get so cold that they acted crazy. They hallucinated and sometimes even thought they were too hot and tore off their clothing. "Spaced out" had been his exact words. He had said that sometimes they just lay down and died.

She told herself to keep moving, if only to stay a little

warmer, and to stay focused. She repeated it over and over: Keep moving. Stay focused. Stay alive.

Nick must be looking for her. She had outsmarted him, but now she had to find a way to outrun him, too. The rough ground slowed her too much. She forced herself to leave the cover of the brush and hobbled out onto the road. The sun was higher. Cindy might be waking up by now. Maybe someone would start looking for her soon.

She laughed bitterly. Looking where? They had the whole world to search. No one had any reason to think Marissa was in the mountains between Portland and the coast. It was up to her to get herself home.

She examined the trees overhanging the road. She didn't know how far the water had taken her. If she could locate the green ribbon, she could guess where she was. There was no sign of the ribbon or note. That was good. The river must have carried her beyond it. She trudged crookedly over the uneven ground.

Could that have been a car? She must have imagined it. Probably her mind was playing tricks on her already. Marissa tried to ignore the sound, but it persisted. Someone was driving up the road toward her. Her heart jumped with hope, then plummeted. What if it was Nick? She dove for the underbrush.

A bright red pickup careened around a bend in the road ahead. It jerked and jostled over the rutted ground. Music blared. This far in the coast range it had to be a tape or CD. Radio reception would be lousy.

The driver was clearly visible through the window. He wore

a kerchief around his head and sunglasses. Three earrings dangled from his right earlobe. A passenger tilted his head back to drain a beer can, then rolled the window down. Music saturated the forest.

Marissa shouted, but they didn't hear her above the deep bass beat of their speakers. She pushed through the shrubs to the road too late. They jolted by within a yard of her. The beer can landed at her feet.

She kicked it viciously and kept walking. At least it was a truck with people in it, and on Thanksgiving Day. Where there was one, there might be another.

Could it be? She *did* hear another car. This one was coming from upriver. She turned and held out her arms, not even thinking about what an alarming sight she must be with her wet curls, her bare feet, and her body partly concealed by a sheet of mottled plastic. She stood in the middle of the road. She wasn't going to let this rescuer get by.

The car was a familiar blue sedan.

Marissa dove for the edge of the road and scrambled out of sight before Nick could slam on his brakes and get out of his car. She stumbled into dense undergrowth. Limber branches whipped her face. Rocks stabbed her bare feet. Still she ran.

He called to her from the road. His coaxing voice was syrupy. "Girl. Girl-o! You come back now, hear?"

Marissa pulled in great gulps of air and stumbled forward. The road curved and sloped sharply down around the edge of a hill. She stood on a steep bank above the curve, with the roadbed about twenty feet below. She could never get down it.

She turned, trapped. Nick crashed through the forest, too close for her to escape.

Marissa braced herself. She had the knife, and she had gained a little understanding of Nick. She raised her head high and opened the knife, holding it down at her side.

"I will not be your next victim," she shouted. "I will not let you hurt me."

Nick halted his headlong rush and gaped at her.

"You're the worst human being I've ever known!" she shouted. "You're a friendless, worthless, hopeless wimp. I pity you!"

He didn't move. Marissa played her last card.

She glared at him and said in an icy voice, "You have been very, very bad. You will have to be punished."

Nick lunged. She struck out with the knife. She felt it pierce his arm. He screamed and jerked. The knife flew out of her hand, and Nick, his arms spinning in wild circles, fell off the bank. His body thudded like a sack of wet sand when it landed on the road below, and she heard a loud snap, then an awful cry of pain.

He kept screaming. Marissa crept to the edge and looked down. He lay with one leg twisted beneath him at an impossible angle.

He flung his head back and his eyes met hers. His screams stopped and he shuddered; then he smiled up at her with his blue eyes flashing and his dimple tracing a perfect vertical line on his chin. His raven hair shone in the morning sunlight.

"Help me, Marissa. I'm hurt. I need a friend. Please, help me?"

Marissa felt sick. Terror and cold had drained her. She turned away in silence and retraced her steps until she could manage the slope.

His car stood with its door open. She looked inside, but Nick had taken his keys. The warm interior tempted her and she struggled with an urge to creep inside. She stopped herself. What if Nick somehow crawled back? The haven began to look more like a prison. She turned and started down the road.

When she reached the curve on the downhill slope, she watched warily. He must be close. Sure enough, she could see the spot where he had lain. Scuff marks showed where he had dragged himself into the forest.

Marissa shrugged and continued down the hill.

She had no idea how long she had been walking. Her vision blurred and each step pounded needles into her aching leg. She just kept going. It was all she could do.

The shivering had started again, and the only sound she heard was her own teeth chattering. Ahead in the road she saw a deer.

No. Her confusion grew. She blinked to clear her vision. It wasn't shaped like a deer. It must be a bear. An alarm shrieked in her numbed brain. What if it was Nick?

She stumbled in a half-circle and tried to hobble in the other direction. Lights flashed all around her. She must be hallucinating.

The bear called her name. Maybe she was finally home at Salmon Creek. Maybe it was a carousel bear. Marissa stood very still and let the bear enfold her in its arms.

Chapter

32

"We've got her. She has a bit of hypothermia, but she ought to be all right. We'll have her at St. Vincent Hospital in about thirty-five minutes."

Officer Barlow signed off the radio and backed his patrol car into a small clearing, then drove down the logging road toward the coast highway. "We'll have you warm and cozy soon, young lady. You've been through a lot."

Marissa wasn't shivering so much. The officer had wrapped her in blankets and settled her in the car with the heater blowing. Others had left in a second car to look for Nick. They hadn't asked her many questions. There would be time for that later.

"We were just catching on that the Parker kid was a false lead." Officer Barlow spoke with easygoing calm. His voice reassured her as much as his words. "When your friend called, we sent out radio bulletins right away. If we hadn't had that radio alert out, the folks who found your note might not have taken it quite so seriously. But they heard about you as soon as they got back toward town, and gave us a call."

He gave her an admiring glance. "Tying that note to a tree was a smart thing to do, but it must have taken some serious guts."

"I didn't feel brave at all. It was more like serious desperation," Marissa said. "I didn't have a lot of choices."

"Guts count most when you're out of choices," he said. "Anyway, they were out looking for a Christmas tree. They found your message this morning before dawn. They figured it wasn't a practical joke because of the diamond ring tied to it. That was a clever touch. You saved your own skin, it looks like."

Marissa laid her head back against the seat and closed her eyes. A single tear flowed across her cheek.

Five months later, Cindy and Marissa leaned on the fence and watched the carousel turn. "Humoresque" poured from the band organ. The music was punctuated by the sound of laughter, which Marissa recognized as Joyful.

Uncle Paul's voice came to them from the shop. "Now this was a really rare find: a Looff camel in not-too-bad condition. I found two horses on that trip, too. We're going to fix them up and put them on an all-Looff carousel down in Oakland. These animals need each other's company, you know. They can die of pure loneliness."

The freshman class sold refreshments from the Snack Shack. Marissa had winced when she recognized one of the boys who had played the Rating Game last fall, but he was busy filling orders and making change. He didn't pay any attention to her, and she allowed him the same courtesy.

"I'd say the First Annual Spring Picnic is an absolute success," Cindy said. "The whole school has you to thank for it."

"I think Gloria would approve," Marissa answered. "She wanted to do this. I wish she could see what a good idea she had."

"It was a good idea to get you on the Student Council, too," Cindy said softly. "There isn't anyone else she would have wanted to finish her term."

Marissa twisted her mother's ring slowly and blinked away an unbidden image of Gloria's ring and Gloria's grave. She knew she would never be entirely free of the things she had seen and experienced at Nick's shack.

"At least you stopped that monster." Cindy's voice was fierce. "He'll never hurt anyone again."

"Humoresque" gave way to "The Beer Barrel Polka." Uncle Paul had, at Marissa's request, omitted "The Carousel Waltz" from the music program. The crowded carousel turned, and Ramona came into view, riding Jewel. She grinned and waved down at them. Jewel's bridle sported a huge red stone.

"You picked the perfect name for Jewel," Marissa said. "Out here in the sunlight, she sparkles."

"Not just on the romance side, either," Cindy commented. "I put a little extra on the side you don't see."

Marissa straightened to her full height. Her green dress fell just below her knees. It brushed gently against her legs as she and Cindy walked together to the main gate to greet a crowd of newcomers. She kept her head high. In a quiet voice she said, "That's the side that counts."

ABOUT THE AUTHOR

Sharon E. Heisel was born and raised in Minnesota. After receiving a master's degree in invertebrate zoology from Portland State University, she taught seventh and eighth grade for eight years, then went on to work as a weight-management counselor. Currently a full-time writer, Sharon Heisel is the author of two children's novels and numerous articles for adults' and children's magazines. *Eyes of a Stranger* is her first young adult novel. She and her husband, Manville, live in Central Point, Oregon, where they enjoy long hikes and frequent carousel rides.